"Ann

"Dean," she whispered in return, her voice that musical, far-off litany that haunted him, waking and dreaming. She caressed his face, then moved her hands to stroke his shoulders, his bare chest, his stomach. She explored every exposed inch of him, anointing him with those fleeting, stimulating kisses.

"Anna," he bit out from between his teeth. "I want you."

"I know," she murmured sadly. "I wish—"

He fought the encroaching drugged sleepiness. "Don't go," he muttered. "Stay with me."

She laid her fingertips against his lips. "I can't. I have to go now."

Before he could respond, she was gone. He groaned and covered his eyes with his arm.

God help him, he'd fallen in love. With a ghost. Perhaps that was only fitting for a man who'd never believed in either.

"I've always wanted to write a book around Valentine's Day," remarks bestselling author **Gina Wilkins**. "Not just a regular Valentine's book, but one with a twist." In *A Valentine Wish*, Gina has done just that. This story has everything: romance, gothic twists, mystery and suspense and terrific characters. Enjoy Dean and Anna's story. And be sure to watch for Ian's story, #592 *A Wish for Love*, coming to Temptation in June.

Books by Gina Wilkins

HARLEQUIN TEMPTATION

Gina Wilkins
A VALENTINE WISH

Harlequin Books

TORONTO • NEW YORK • LONDON
AMSTERDAM • PARIS • SYDNEY • HAMBURG
STOCKHOLM • ATHENS • TOKYO • MILAN
MADRID • WARSAW • BUDAPEST • AUCKLAND

ISBN 0-373-25676-0

A VALENTINE WISH

Copyright © 1996 by Gina Wilkins.

Printed in U.S.A.

Prologue

There is only one happiness in life, to love and be loved.

—George Sand

February 14, 1896

IT WAS dark outside, and cold. The wind moaned around the walls as though begging to be allowed inside and tiny pellets of ice tapped incessantly against the heavily curtained windows. In contrast, the bedroom was stiflingly warm, with an enormous fire roaring in the hearth and lamps burning brightly on the papered walls.

The woman in the bed lay limply against the pillows, cradling a sleeping baby in each arm. Her eyes wet with tears, she looked from one tiny, innocent face to the other. This was the first time since their birth several hours earlier that she'd been alone with them, and she'd had to almost beg to be granted this brief respite from all the well-intentioned assistance.

"Ian," she whispered, kissing the downy soft forehead of her firstborn, who lay nestled in her left arm.

She turned her head to the right and placed another loving kiss against the second tiny forehead. "Mary

Anna," she murmured. "My angels. How I love you both. If only your dear father—"

She choked on her words, and the tears overflowed, cascading down her pale cheeks. She was twenty-three years old, widowed three months and left with a bustling inn to run and two tiny babies to raise. She did not know how she would manage, but somehow she knew she would.

She must.

She lifted her teary gaze to the portrait that hung on the wall opposite the bed, the first thing she saw each morning, the last she looked at every night before she slept. "I'll take care of them, James," she promised her beloved late husband. "I will raise them to be strong and honorable, just as you would have wanted them raised."

She looked down at her babies once more. "I have no magical powers, my darlings," she murmured to them. "But if I did, I would say an incantation for you now. My gift to you would be that of true love—the pure and lasting love I found so briefly with your father. I would cast a spell that would guarantee you would not leave this earth until you each found someone who would love you the way James loved me—and whom you could love that deeply in return."

Again, her gaze rose to the portrait. "Help me, James," she whispered. "Help me give them that gift, above all others."

The words were a prayer.

In the fireplace, the flames suddenly intensified— fanned, perhaps, by a stray breeze. Whatever the cause, the resulting light glowed bright and hot on the portrait, making the painted man's dark eyes gleam as they had in life, with intelligence, humor and a deep, abiding love.

His wife let out a faint, longing sob. And then the flames subsided, the portrait dimmed and little Ian stirred, whimpering softly. His mother turned her attention to her son, but she would never forget that brief, magical moment when her wish seemed to have been heard and acknowledged.

February 14, 1921

IT WAS COLD in the garden, and dark. No moonlight or starlight was visible through the gray clouds overhead. The only illumination came through the windows of the inn. Inside, a party raged. Faint strains of music and laughter filtered through the glass, underscoring the contrast between the gaiety inside and the peacefulness of the garden.

Mary Anna Cameron shivered as she stepped outside. She hadn't had a chance to get her coat, but had slipped away from the party at the first opportunity, afraid that someone would detain her. Jeffrey, her fiancé, would soon notice her absence, and would come looking for her. She hoped to have a chance to talk to her brother in private before they were interrupted.

She found her twin furiously pacing the brick path, his lethally graceful movements held under such tight control, she knew his temper must be close to explosion point. She'd expected to find him here. Ian always came to the gardens when his vexation got the best of him. Anna was probably the only person who wasn't afraid of his notorious temper.

"Ian?" she said softly.

He turned to face her. Like the heavy clouds above them, the frown that creased his dark face threatened a potential storm. "Go back inside, Anna. Find your devoted fiancé. Enjoy your party."

"It's *our* party, Ian. Yours and mine. Please don't spoil it."

He exhaled impatiently. "I'm in no mood for a birthday party."

"Ian, please. The rumors don't matter."

"How can you say that? Haven't you seen the way people have been looking at me this evening? Whispering behind my back? Don't you know what they're saying? It doesn't bother you that I'm being accused of bootlegging? That I'm being labeled a murderer?"

"Of course it bothers me," she said sharply. "I hate it that anyone could think so low of you. But I keep reminding myself that no one who really knows you could believe such drivel."

"I've seen the way people have been watching me the past two weeks. There are quite a few of them who *do* believe the drivel."

"They're wrong." Her chin lifted with loyal obstinance. "Sheriff Fielding will find out who killed that revenue officer. Your name will be cleared, and everyone who ever suspected you will be forced to apologize."

He shook his head. "Sheriff Fielding would just as soon lock me up as not. As for the others—most of them would rather choke than apologize to me for anything. You seem to forget that I'm not the most popular guy around these parts."

"If only you'd give them a chance to know you," she said wistfully.

"They know me, Anna. They just don't like me."

She sighed, unable to argue with him. Her brother's prickly temper had gained him too few friends and all too many adversaries. It bothered her that Ian always seemed so alone, that she was the only one who truly understood him. And, though he would never admit it, she suspected that it sometimes bothered him, too.

She moved to Ian's side and slid her hand through the crook of his arm, keeping her voice soft, gentling. Calming him as only she could. "Forget about the gossip mongers. They don't matter. Today is our twenty-fifth birthday and the inn is now ours to manage as we choose. You no longer have to sit back and watch Gaylon make decisions that you don't like. You can make those changes you've been dying to make for the past five years, and there's nothing our stepfather—or anyone else—can do to stop you. Doesn't that make you feel better?"

He slowed his steps, matching them to hers as they wandered down the path, unhindered by the lack of light. They'd been born in the back bedroom of this inn, had lived every day of their lives here. Both of them loved the place with an intensity that few others had ever understood. They could have made their way blindfolded.

Anna could feel some of the tension leave Ian's arm as her words sank in.

"Yes," he admitted. "You know how I've looked forward to this day."

"How we've *both* looked forward to it," she corrected him. "Mother thought she was making the best decision for everyone to name Gaylon the executor of her will until we turned twenty-five, but it has been difficult watching the mistakes he's made running the inn. I'm sure he's tried his best, but—"

"But he's a fool."

She sighed at her brother's curt interruption. "He's simply not particularly skilled at management," she said. "At least, not in the way you and I would choose to run our inn."

"At a profit, you mean?"

"You can make the inn profitable again once you're in charge. Providing, of course," she added with an indulgent smile, "you don't turn away all the guests with your tantrums."

"I don't throw tantrums," he protested, sounding a bit stung by the gentle criticism.

She chuckled. "Of course you do, darling. Why, Jeffrey is half-terrified of you."

Ian's snort effectively expressed his opinion of her somewhat timid fiancé, an opinion he'd never made much effort to conceal. Anna knew Ian thought she could do better than Jeffrey Parker, a mild-mannered young banker with soft hands and a nervous habit of clearing his throat. But Anna was fond of Jeffrey, and thought he would make a loyal, biddable husband and a doting father.

She had informed Ian that she'd grown tired of waiting for that mythical, passionate love their mother had spoken of so often. Anna was twenty-five years old now, and she'd had few other offers to choose from. She loved children, and wanted several of them. She couldn't afford to wait any longer.

Besides, she had added tersely, she wasn't sure she wanted to be desperately in love with anyone. Their mother had apparently loved their father that way, and she'd never truly recovered from his untimely death. She'd married again, several years after James Cameron died, but though she'd been a good wife to Gaylon

Peavy, she'd never gotten over her grief for her first husband.

Anna was much too independent to allow herself to become that attached to anyone—except, perhaps, her beloved twin.

The inn was well behind them now, the sounds of the party muted. The two were content to be alone, strolling the grounds where they'd spent so many happy hours as children. This was their home, their legacy from the father they'd never known and the mother they'd adored. From the day they'd been born, it had been theirs, though only now could they fully claim it.

Ian's dark suit blended into the shadows around them, but Anna thought her own long, straight white dress made her look like a ghost gliding down the pathway. The image amused her, and she smiled.

"It's you Jeffrey should truly worry about," Ian said after a moment, interrupting Anna's fanciful thoughts. "You're much too strong-willed for him. You'll order him about and manipulate him for the rest of his life."

"I am not a shrew!"

"No," he admitted with a hint of humor. "You'll do it so nicely, he'll probably never know just how tightly you hold the reins. There's a good chance that he'll actually be quite happy, blithely assuming he's the head of his household."

"Of course he'll be happy. I'll be a good wife to him, Ian."

"Yes. I only hope that you will be happy, as well. You're absolutely sure you want to commit yourself to this man?"

"I'm sure," she said gently, resting her head against his shoulder as they walked. "But thank you for caring."

"I do care."

She smiled mistily. "Because you love me."

"Yes." His voice was gruff, as it always was when he attempted to verbalize his inner feelings. "You're the only one in this world I do love, Anna. Nothing is more important to me than your happiness. Not even the inn."

She blinked back tears. It was so rare for her brother to express himself that way. The words were all the more precious to her because she knew they'd been difficult for him to say. "I love you, too, Ian. I—"

He shushed her suddenly, coming to an abrupt halt, his attention focused on something ahead of them.

"What is it?" she asked, keeping her voice low.

"There's a light in the old caretaker's cottage. Someone's in there."

Startled, Anna peered through the shadows. After a moment, she saw a flicker of light in the direction Ian indicated. A lantern, perhaps. There was no electricity in the old cottage at the edge of the woods. The cottage was at the back of the inn's grounds and had been unoccupied for the past ten years or more. No one should be there now.

"A hobo, do you think?" she asked in a whisper.

"Maybe," Ian muttered. "Whoever it is, he has no business being here. You go back to the inn. I'll run him off."

Her grasp tightened on his arm. "No. It could be dangerous for you alone. Go back and find Gaylon and some of the others to help you."

He shook off her hand and started toward the cottage. "I don't need Gaylon. I can handle this."

"Ian." She hurried after him, stumbling a bit without his support. "Wait."

Both of them saw the three men who emerged suddenly from the cottage. One of them held a lantern, his face clearly illuminated. Anna gasped in relief when she recognized Stanley Tagert, a local police officer. She couldn't yet identify the other two men, who stood in the shadows behind Tagert, but she was glad to know that Ian wouldn't be facing a potentially dangerous stranger.

She didn't particularly like Stanley—she'd never cared for the way he looked at her—but he was an officer of the law, and surely quite capable of taking care of trespassers on Cameron property.

"Stanley," she said, stepping forward. "What are you—"

Ian moved suddenly, sharply. "Anna, wait—"

A flash of light, accompanied by a startlingly loud noise, came from the direction of the shadowed man directly behind Tagert. Ian jerked, staggered, then crumpled to the ground.

He didn't move again.

Momentarily paralyzed with horror, Anna hardly registered Tagert's furious oath.

"What the hell did you do that for?" he demanded of the other man. "Have you—"

Staring down at Ian, Anna paid no attention to the words. Finally finding the impetus to move, she threw herself onto the ground next to her brother's motionless form. "Ian? Oh, God, *no!*"

Kneeling beside him, she touched his face with trembling fingers. And knew the truth.

"Ian," she whispered, doubling over in agony. "Oh, Ian. No."

She turned then, to find out who had done this inconceivably brutal thing. Two faces were visible in the lantern light now. Tagert and another man, Buck Felcher, a local troublemaker known for his criminal tendencies. She still couldn't make out the features of the third man, the one who'd fired the shot that had killed her brother.

"Stanley," she said, her voice a shaken whisper. "Buck. Why? *Why?*"

She heard the second shot even as the impact caught her in the chest and threw her backward, away from Ian's body. Two angry shouts erupted simultaneously, followed by a third shot and a distant thud.

Oblivious to the pain and the chaos surrounding her, aware only of the new layers of darkness wrapping themselves around her, Anna strained to reach out, feeling as though she were moving through a pool of molasses. Her fingers brushed her twin's wrist. She let her hand fall on top of his.

"Ian," she whispered, her voice no more than a tremulous sigh. "Ian . . ."

Then darkness swallowed her.

1

She was a Phantom of delight
When first she gleamed upon my sight
— William Wordsworth

January 3, 1996

DEAN GATES, new owner of the soon-to-be-restored Cameron Inn, didn't believe in ghosts. So it was all the more annoying when he saw one less than an hour after moving into his new home.

He stood in the center of the mildew-scented, dimly lit attic of the inn, the only part he'd yet to fully explore. He'd just made a quick survey of the stacks of old junk and boxes that had been stashed up here for who knew how long. He added them to his long mental list of things to take care of as he began his renovations.

Preoccupied with that list, he ran a hand through his brown hair and made a slow circle in the center of the room, scanning the rafters for signs of weakness or water damage, half his attention focused on his growing hunger. He hadn't eaten anything since a light breakfast some eight hours earlier.

The ghost was standing in one corner of the attic, watching him with a distinctly curious expression.

Dean blinked. He was absolutely certain that corner had been empty only moments ago. Now it was occupied by a slender woman in a long white dress that made him think of flappers and rumble seats. Her hair was dark, chin-length, crimped into stylized waves around her beautiful face. She had large dark eyes, flawless fair skin, a slightly dimpled chin and a rosy mouth that looked tailor-made for kissing. She was, without doubt, the most stunning woman Dean had ever seen.

He couldn't quite believe he was seeing her now.

He reached up to rub his eyes, thinking perhaps it was a trick of the shadows, a manifestation of his weariness after a long drive, maybe even a hallucination brought on by hunger. When he opened his eyes again, she was still there, looking at him with a slight frown creasing her forehead.

Deciding she was a trespasser who'd somehow slipped into the attic without him hearing her, he opened his mouth to ask who she was...and then closed it abruptly when he realized he could see the walls of the room through her dress. Through *her*.

"Oh, man," he said, his voice sounding husky in the silence of the attic. "I need something to eat."

He turned on one heel and headed for the stairwell. "Aunt Mae?" he called out as he took the stairs two at a time. "Hey, Aunt Mae? Let's go have some lunch, okay?"

ANNA TURNED quickly to her brother. "Ian, I think he saw us!"

Ian didn't look so sure. "He must have seen *something* that startled him."

"He was looking right at us."

"No. He was looking at you."

Anna waved off the distinction.

"You know, it was odd," she mused aloud, gazing toward the staircase which the man had so abruptly descended. "I had the strangest sensation when he looked at me. Almost as if—as if I could have spoken with him, if I'd tried. He didn't seem as far away as the others."

She knew she didn't have to explain. Ian was all too aware of those invisible barriers that stood between them and the mortals they'd occasionally encountered during the passing years. Only rarely had the barriers lowered enough for the others to see Anna and her brother, and on those occasions the contact had been extremely brief and decidedly unsatisfying.

But this time . . . this time it had felt different.

"Maybe I should have said something," she murmured.

"Even if he'd heard you—and I'm not at all sure that he would have—he would have merely screamed and taken to his heels," Ian responded cynically. "The way all the others have when they've spotted us."

For some reason, Anna was annoyed by his presumption. "He didn't look so fainthearted to me. There's something different about him, Ian. Something . . . I don't know . . ."

Frustrated by her lack of words, she grimaced. She could still picture the man's face, strong-boned, firm-jawed, not quite handsome, but definitely intriguing. And his eyes—a deep, piercing blue. Eyes that saw much and betrayed little. "He had kind eyes," she murmured. "Maybe he's the one who can help us—if only we can find a way to talk to him."

Ian snorted, typically impatient with her fancifulness. "He's just like the others, Anna. He bought the inn on a whim, and now he'll throw too little money into it, too little interest, and when he becomes bored or financially strapped—as they all do eventually—he'll abandon it. No one really cares about this place. And no one cares about us."

Anna tossed her head in annoyance at his pessimism. "Don't talk like that! We're here for a reason, Ian. I've always believed that someday, someone would come along who would help free us. This man could be the one."

Ian's eyes softened as he looked at her. "You always have been the dreamer."

She smiled back at him. "And you the doubter. We shall just have to see who is right, won't we?"

His own faint smile faded. "It's not as though we have anything better to do," he muttered.

Ignoring the underlying bitterness in his tone, Anna turned away and looked at the staircase again, wondering how she could communicate with the man with the kind blue eyes.

TWENTY MINUTES after leaving the attic, Dean stepped out of his car and glanced around his new hometown. Destiny, Arkansas. Population 5,462—a number he mentally amended to 5,464 now that he and his aunt Mae had arrived.

From the sidewalk where he stood on the east side of Main Street, he could see the two-story, white brick city hall building, the tiny redbrick post office, a convenience store with four gas pumps in front, the aging native-stone building that housed the local newspaper, *Destiny Daily,* three churches of different denominations, several less-than-flourishing retail establishments and what appeared to be a thriving video-rental store. The Destiny Diner was behind him, where only a few customers remained inside since it was a couple of hours past the usual lunch hour.

Tired Christmas decorations drooped from posts and window frames. Dean suspected they'd been up since shortly after Halloween. There was nothing more dispirited-looking than Christmas decorations in January, he thought wryly.

"I'm starving," his aunt Mae said fervently, moving to stand beside him. "We must stop by a grocery store on the way home so we'll have supplies for dinner this evening."

Dean smiled at his comfortably plump, sixty-year-old maternal aunt. She was an eccentric-looking woman, with her profusion of jangling bracelets, dangling oversize earrings and enormous, stuffed-to-overflowing purse. Her fuchsia sweater clashed cheerfully with her copper-dyed hair, her black slacks were a bit too tight and her eyeglasses were a godawful design of gold wires, red plastic and tiny rhinestones. Dean was well aware that beneath the unusual exterior was a sharp mind, an even sharper wit and a generously loving heart.

He was crazy about her.

Inside the diner, Dean and Mae were greeted by an ample young woman in jeans and an Arkansas Razorbacks sweatshirt. "Table for two?" she asked while chewing on a piece of gum. "Smoking or non?" she continued before they could answer her first question.

Dean glanced ruefully at the small, one-room diner, in which none of the tables was more than a foot or two apart. "Nonsmoking," he said, deciding to hope for the best.

The tables were decorated with red paper hearts and red and white silk carnations. The decorations were still clean and appeared to be new, making Dean suspect that someone had replaced the Christmas trappings that very morning. It wasn't hard to imagine that these would soon look as tired and worn-out as the garland and tinsel he'd noticed outside.

"They've already decorated for Valentine's Day," Aunt Mae said as she took her seat. "It will be here almost before we know it, I suppose."

Dean picked up a plastic-coated menu and muttered something noncommittal. Valentine's Day was not a topic that interested him in the least.

Mae sighed. "You should have someone special to celebrate the occasion with."

He forced a smile. "I do have someone special. You."

"That's not what I meant and you know it. I'm talking about a significant other, or whatever they call them these days. Just because your marriage didn't work out is no reason to cut yourself off from all romantic possibilities in the future. You're only thirty-five. There's still plenty of time for you to fall in love and have a family."

"We've had this conversation before. Many times. Don't start it again, please."

She sighed again. "I can't help it. I've always loved Valentine's Day. My Walter never let one pass without fanfare."

"My ex-wife never let one pass without fanfare, either," Dean said dryly. "The occasion always cost me a fortune in roses and diamonds, not because I particularly wanted to buy them, but because I knew she'd sulk for at least a month if I didn't. The whole charade is just a bunch of bull, as far as I'm concerned, dreamed up by jewelers, florists and greeting-card companies."

"So cynical," Mae murmured sadly, watching him with eyes as blue and perceptive as his own. "Gloria burned you very badly, didn't she? I wonder at times if the scars will ever heal."

Dean was relieved when the waitress reappeared to take their orders. As much as he loved his aunt, her unabashed romanticism sometimes made him uncomfortable. He was the practical, pragmatic type, himself. The most audacious and quixotic thing Dean had ever done was to leave a six-figure-a-year marketing career to buy a picturesque old run-down inn in central Arkansas.

He'd told himself it hadn't been as capricious as it had sounded. Dean's grandfather—Mae's father—had been a hotelier, operating a moderately successful small chain that he'd eventually sold to a national conglomerate. Dean had always been fascinated by his grandfather's career, and had thought it was something he might like to do himself. He'd drifted into marketing almost by accident, but the hotel business had always intrigued him.

He'd seen the Cameron Inn pictured in a real-estate ad in a business magazine he'd been reading during a particularly long, boring airplane trip after a particularly long, boring business trip. Something about the photo had captured his attention—and then hadn't released it. Within a week after seeing the ad, he'd found himself on another airplane, this one headed to Arkansas. He'd told himself that he only wanted to look the place over, with an eye for a possible investment opportunity.

Six months later, the inn was his. Any excuses he might make for his actions notwithstanding, the truth was, he'd taken one look at the place and had known he had to have it.

Even then, he'd tried to convince himself that the decision hadn't been totally impulsive and impractical.

Tourism was growing in this area, located in the naturally beautiful hill country only a few miles north of Hot Springs National Park, and the inn should do well, once Dean restored it to its former elegance and established a reputation for fine cuisine and restful accommodations. Despite what some people were saying about him lately, he hadn't completely lost his mind when he'd made the decision to pursue a new direction in life.

He couldn't even imagine what those same people would say if they learned that he'd seen a ghost on the very first day of his new career. The thought made him wince.

"Dean? Is something wrong with your food?" his aunt asked as the waitress walked away after bringing them their meals.

He cleared his expression and shook his head. "No, it's fine. Quite good, actually," he assured her, taking a bite of chicken-fried steak smothered in cream gravy, and ignoring the twinges of his nutritional conscience.

A tall, lanky man with sandy brown hair and smiling green eyes stopped by their table on his way out of the diner. "You must be the new owners of the Cameron Inn."

"My nephew is the new owner," Mae replied. "This is Dean Gates. And I'm Mae Harper, his first official employee."

The man smiled. "Nice to meet you both. I'm Mark Winter, owner and publisher of the local newspaper, the *Destiny Daily*. Welcome to town."

"Thanks," Dean said. "Sign me up for a subscription to your paper. I'll want to keep up with the town news."

Winter's mouth kicked up in a lazy, rueful smile. "Oh, we cover all the big events. Just this morning, I received an invitation to cover the Destiny Elementary School's annual St. Valentine's Day Pageant next weekend. A hundred of our youngest and finest citizens plan to recite poems by Elizabeth Barrett Browning and Rod McKuen and mangle—er—perform pop love songs. It should be inspirational. You have to experience it to truly appreciate it. Why don't you plan to attend?"

Dean managed not to shudder. "Sounds...enthralling. I'll have to check my calendar."

Winter chuckled. "Do you have children to add to our local talent pool?"

"No. I'm not married."

"Me, neither," Winter admitted. "Things like this always remind me why."

Dean grinned.

Aunt Mae sighed and muttered something about "bachelors."

"Say, would you mind if I interview you once you've had a chance to settle in?" Winter asked Dean. "The townsfolk are always interested in new residents. And they'll be particularly curious since you'll be restoring the old Cameron place."

"I'm not sure there's that much of interest to tell them."

"Of course there is. Your plans for the place. What made you decide to move here. Anything you'd like to tell us about your background." His smile turned mischievous. "How you feel about ghosts."

Dean nearly overturned his water glass. He steadied it quickly. "Er—ghosts?"

"You *were* told that the Cameron Inn is haunted, weren't you? It's one of the favorite legends around these parts."

"The real-estate agent mentioned the rumors in passing," Dean admitted. "I told her I wasn't particularly interested. I don't believe in ghosts," he added firmly.

His aunt was looking at him with wide, indignant eyes. "You knew the inn was supposed to be haunted and you didn't tell me?"

Winter looked suddenly uncomfortable. "Sorry," he said to her. "I assumed you'd already heard. I hope I haven't worried you. I assure you, it's only a—"

"Wouldn't it be wonderful to see a real ghost?" Aunt Mae interrupted with a blissful look of anticipation. "What fun! Think how good this will be for your business, Dean. Once the tourists find out the place is actually *haunted* . . ."

Dean rolled his eyes. "Aunt Mae, I want guests to come to our inn because it's restful and comfortable and efficiently run. I want to provide a place for them to get away from the bustle and stress of everyday life, a place for lovers and honeymooners to take long, peaceful walks in the woods, return for an exquisitely prepared meal and then retire to the privacy of their own tastefully furnished rooms. I do not want to attract a mob of crystal-carrying, New Age ghost-groupies."

Winter chuckled. "Ghost-groupies. I like it."

"Well, I don't," Dean muttered. "I don't believe in ghosts," he repeated, shoving aside an eerie mental image of a beautiful dark-haired woman in a long, white dress. A hunger hallucination, he reminded himself. Nothing more.

"Yeah, well, I'll give you a call about that interview."

Dean forced a smile. "Sure. Anytime."

Winter ambled away. A man in a dark gray suit that hung oddly around his thin frame approached the table just as Dean and Mae finished their meals. "I'm Mayor Charles Peavy Vandover," he said, the name rolling majestically off his tongue. "Welcome to our town."

Dean offered a hand. "Thank you. I'm Dean Gates, and this is my aunt, Mae Harper."

The mayor, who appeared to be in his mid-forties, shook Dean's hand and nodded politely at Mae. "I've heard of you, of course. Glad to have a chance to meet you. We're always pleased when new business comes to our area."

Vandover jerked his head toward the door, through which Mark Winter had exited a short time ago. "I was sitting at the next table and I couldn't help overhearing some of what Winter was telling you. I hope you didn't take all that garbage about the ghost legend seriously. Every town has its foolish rumors, of course, but we've never encouraged that sort of folderol around here. It isn't good for our image, if you know what I mean."

"I was just telling Winter that I have no intention of making an issue of the legend," Dean said firmly. "Many old buildings have such rumors connected to them. Once the inn is restored and we're doing business, I'm confident that we'll put the legend to rest."

The mayor nodded in satisfaction. "I look forward to holding a ribbon-cutting ceremony when you're ready to open. My great-grandfather once owned that inn, and his son after him. My family has strong ties to the place."

Dean lifted an eyebrow. "I wasn't aware of that."

"Never been a hint of scandal connected to our name," Vandover added flatly. "Any rumors you might hear to the contrary are just that. Unfounded rumors. Don't you listen to 'em, you hear?"

"Er—sure." Dean decided right then to find out exactly what "rumors" were connected to his inn. He needed to be prepared. Maybe Mark Winter could supply him with details in exchange for an interview.

THE WAITRESS in the Razorbacks sweatshirt took Dean's money at the cash register. "I heard what the mayor said," she commented, making Dean think ruefully that eavesdropping seemed to be an acceptable hobby around here. "About the ghosts?"

"What about them, dear?" Mae asked when Dean would have let the subject drop without comment.

"They're real, all right. My mom knew someone once who knew someone who saw them."

"Them?" Mae repeated avidly as Dean suppressed a sigh.

The young woman nodded. "There's two of 'em. A man and a woman. S'posed to be twins."

Dean almost groaned at that. Not only was he expected to believe his inn was haunted by ghosts, he had *twin* ghosts. Great.

"If you're going to see 'em, it'll prob'ly be on Valentine's Day," the woman added. "It's their birthday. And the day they died."

"Valentine ghosts," Mae said with a sigh, her eyes gleaming impishly. "Isn't that romantic, Dean?"

He muttered something incomprehensible, threw some money on the counter and left the diner with little more than a grudgingly polite nod at the waitress.

"I don't know about you," Mae murmured as they climbed into the car. "But now I'm more curious about the ghosts than ever."

"We've got a lot more to worry about than ghosts. Plumbing and wiring, dry rot, modernizing the kitchen, refurbishing all the rooms. Paint, wallpaper, carpeting, wood to be stripped and resealed, fixtures to replace..."

Mae smiled. "It's going to be great fun, isn't it, Dean?"

He relaxed enough to return her smile. "Yes," he said. "I think it will."

HAVING FULLY EXPLORED the inside of the inn, Dean concentrated on the outside while his aunt put away the groceries they'd purchased on the way home.

The sprawling two-story structure opened into a large lobby and reception area, with the public dining room off to the right. The kitchen, a smaller dining room, four small bedrooms, two baths and a private sitting room were at the back of the ground floor. The ten guest rooms were on the second floor, each with a tiny, but adequate, private bathroom not much larger than a walk-in closet. Above that, of course, was the attic.

Dean didn't want to think about the attic right now.

Built in 1892 by James Cameron, a British immigrant, the inn was country-style, with multiple shuttered windows and dormers, and an inviting wraparound porch. It had been mostly unoccupied for the past six years. Some of the windows were cracked, shutters were crooked, paint was peeling and faded and boards were splintered and rotted in places.

A few renovations had been made over the years, but general neglect had finally taken its toll. The grounds were a mess of dead weeds, sprawling bushes and un-pruned, winter-denuded trees. The driveway was rutted, the footpaths broken and uneven, and the once-flourishing garden was overgrown and run-down.

Dean looked at the place and saw the simple elegance that had once been, the same look he hoped to achieve again.

So far, only the kitchen, two of the back bedrooms and the private sitting room were habitable. Freshly painted, papered and furnished with antiques and re-productions, the rooms had been decorated according to Dean's instructions while he'd finished up his business in Chicago during the past month. He had considered the private living quarters the first priority; after all, he and Mae would be making this their home.

Stuffing his hands into the pockets of his heavy jacket, he strolled around the side of the building, mentally adding to his list of needed repairs. Had it been summer, the garden path would have been so choked with weeds and vines, walking down it would have been difficult. As it was, he sidestepped the thorny branches that threatened the fabric of his wool slacks.

A rotting, precariously leaning shack that was little more than a stack of old boards lay at the back of the grounds, at the very edge of the woods through which Dean planned to cut nature trails and hiking paths. He'd have to clear away that shack, eventually. It

looked as old as the inn, and had long since deterio-
rated past usefulness.

There were a couple of other dilapidated outbuildings on the property, all of which had to go. He had
vague plans to build a few guest cottages once business
picked up enough to justify the extra investment—
honeymoon cottages, perhaps.

He didn't have to be a romantic to know how to cap-
italize on that human weakness.

It was late afternoon now, and long shadows
stretched across the path in front of him. He had almost reached the old shack, when something made him
stop.

Compared to Chicago at this time of year, it wasn't
a particularly chilly afternoon. The temperature hovered in the low fifties, but Dean was suddenly cold,
right through to the bone. Instinctively, he moved back
a few steps. The coldness went away.

Frowning, Dean moved slowly forward. The coldness hit him again in the very same spot on the path, a
deep, skin-tightening chill that made him decidedly
uneasy. He wasn't standing in a shadow, nor in a low
spot, and there was no other apparent physical explanation as to why it would be colder here than it was five
feet away. But it was.

The hairs at the back of his neck rose with a tickle of
premonition. Reluctantly, warily, he turned.

She was standing on the path right behind him, so
close he could almost touch her.

He kept his hands in his pockets. He had a nagging
suspicion that his fingers would go right through her if
he reached out.

The outline of a straggly, winter-dead rosebush was
dimly visible through her, as though seen through sheer

white fabric. Only her face was perfectly clear—and as beautiful as it had been when he'd seen her in the attic.

"I," he told her stupidly, "do not believe in ghosts."

She smiled. Her mouth moved, but no sound emerged. At least, nothing that he could hear. She looked suddenly frustrated, as though annoyed that he hadn't responded to whatever she'd tried to say.

Which, of course, was ridiculous. "I am *not* going crazy," he said emphatically.

She shook her head, her expression reassuring.

He wasn't reassured.

He thought of the people who'd questioned his sanity when he'd quit his fast-track career in Chicago and announced that he'd bought a run-down old inn in an off-the-beaten-path town in central Arkansas. He thought of his ex-wife's recent telephone call, not so subtly inquiring if he was having a nervous breakdown following their divorce a year ago. Irritably, he'd assured her that he wasn't.

He hoped to hell no one would ask him that question now. He wasn't at all sure he could answer so positively.

"This is absurd," he said, his eyes never leaving the woman's face. "It's a joke, right? A twisted way of welcoming me to town? Someone's idea of having fun with the newcomer? What are you, a projection?"

A look of sympathy crossed her face, overriding what might have been exasperation.

Great. Now even his hallucination felt sorry for him.

He raised his voice a bit. "Whoever is behind this, ha, ha. Great joke. You've really pulled a good one. You must introduce yourself sometime so that I can fully express my appreciation for your inventiveness. And now, if you'll excuse me, I have things to do inside. You can turn off your projector."

The woman didn't leave. She reached out a hand to him, her dark eyes beseeching.

"Great effect," he muttered, shaken despite himself by the appeal in her . . . well, her haunted eyes. "But wouldn't it have been spookier at night?"

He shrugged. "I'll make it easier for you," he said to whoever was listening. "I'll turn around. When I turn back, the 'ghost' will have vanished, okay?"

Her lips moved. He thought she said, "Wait."

He turned. Counted to fifty. Then to seventy-five, just to make sure he'd allowed the prankster plenty of time to comply with his demand. When he turned back, the woman was gone.

Exhaling in relief, Dean briefly considered searching the grounds, finding the practical joker and rearranging his teeth. He restrained the uncharacteristically ferocious impulse with a proud lift of his chin. Dean Gates could take a joke as well as anyone. He wouldn't have his new neighbors snickering and saying otherwise.

"Welcome to Destiny," he muttered, shaking his head as he strode impatiently back to his supposedly haunted inn. "Home of ghosts and fruitcakes."

He sincerely hoped his first day here hadn't set a pattern for the rest of his stay, however long that might be.

"I TOLD YOU he wouldn't be able to hear you," Ian couldn't seem to resist pointing out.

Watching wistfully as the man strode angrily down the path toward the inn, Anna sighed. "At least you have to acknowledge that he saw us that time."

"You," he corrected. "He saw you."

"I'm sure he saw us both. It's just that I was the one trying to speak to him. I was so sure he'd be able to hear me."

"Sweetheart, you are a ghost. He can't hear you. I'm not even sure he really saw you."

"He saw me," Anna insisted stubbornly. "And somehow, I'm going to make him hear me. I just have to try harder next time."

"Anna—"

She whirled on him. "Do you have any better suggestions?" she demanded. "What do you want to do, drift around in limbo for eternity? At least I'm *trying* to free us!"

"I just don't want you to be disappointed. It's hard enough not knowing what happened to us, or why. We don't know why we're here, we don't know what, if anything, can free us—or where we'd go if we could leave."

"*I* know why we're here. I'm certain it's to clear our names, change the lies that we've heard told about us all these years. All we need is someone to help us find out the truth, someone who'll tell everyone what really happened, and we'll be free. It's the only possibility that makes sense to me."

Ian refused to argue with her anymore. After all, they'd been having this same pointless discussion for three-quarters of a century.

Anna turned away. Her brother was as tenacious as the blue-eyed man she'd been trying to talk to. She couldn't help smiling as she thought of the man's adamant insistence that he didn't believe in ghosts, despite the evidence in front of him. He was a stubborn one, she mused.

But then, so was she.

2

Was it a vision, or a waking dream?
—John Keats

DEAN AND MAE had just finished dinner when the old-
fashioned, 1950s-era doorbell clanged, announcing a
caller at the inn's front door. Having hardly touched his
meal, Dean sprang to his feet to answer the summons.

He welcomed the diversion from the disturbing
thoughts that had been troubling him all evening,
making him a less-than-scintillating dinner compan-
ion for his poor, curious aunt.

As he approached the front door, he couldn't help
wondering if the visitor would be the prankster who'd
played such an elaborate trick on him a few hours ago.
Maybe it was someone who would cheerfully claim re-
sponsibility, generously concede that Dean was a good
sport and solemnly promise never to do such a thing
again.

His hopes of discovering the culprit collapsed when
he opened the door. He doubted very much that the
frosted-haired woman standing outside the door, a
covered dish in her hands, had masterminded the elaborate practical joke. "Ms. Burton. Come in," he said,
politely greeting the real-estate agent who'd first shown
him the inn.

Divorced, and in her early thirties, Sharyn Burton
had made no secret of her interest in Dean, to his aunt's

amusement and his own rueful embarrassment. He didn't know what it was about his ordinary face, slightly shaggy brown hair and bright blue eyes that intrigued her, but something obviously did, judging from the way she behaved around him.

"Hi," she said, giving him a toothy smile as she minced past him. "I brought you a peach cobbler to celebrate your first night in the inn."

"That was very thoughtful of you." Dean took the heavy dish from her and then wondered what to do with it—and her.

There was nowhere for her to sit in the lobby, which was empty except for the massive oak reception desk that stretched in front of the back wall—an original fixture of the inn, the realtor had assured him. A once-magnificent Williamsburg chandelier hung over them, giving out just enough light to deepen the shadows in the corners of the lobby. Dean found himself avoiding looking at those shadows, even though he was confident that he would see no one standing in them.

Though he wasn't really in the mood for entertaining, courtesy forced him to invite Sharyn to join him and his aunt in the dining room for dessert. Mae welcomed Sharyn warmly, and rushed to pour her a cup of coffee before going to the kitchen. She returned carrying dishes for the peach cobbler. Both she and Dean made appropriately appreciative comments after tasting the still-warm dessert.

"I'm glad you like it," Sharyn said with a smile that was obviously for Dean's benefit.

He concentrated on his cobbler, hoping this wasn't going to get awkward. Sharyn seemed nice enough, but he had absolutely no interest in dating her. Or anyone else, for that matter. At least not right away.

He found himself wondering inconsequentially about the dark-haired, dark-eyed "ghost." Who was the woman who'd posed for those projections? Was she a local resident? Would Sharyn know her if he described her? He was reluctant to bring up the subject, still smarting from the uneasiness he'd felt before he'd figured out that he was the victim of an elaborate prank.

"I heard you met our mayor this afternoon," Sharyn commented, reclaiming his attention.

Dean looked up in surprise.

Reading his expression, Sharyn gave a sheepish little shrug. "Word gets around quickly here," she explained. "You can hardly sneeze in Destiny without everyone hearing about it."

Dean winced. He'd heard about small-town gossip, but had never actually become the topic of it. Of course, he wasn't so sure it was any different from the corporate-circle gossip he'd endured in Chicago. He would bet tongues were still wagging there about his abrupt decision to move to Arkansas.

"What did you think of the mayor?" Sharyn asked, directing the question to both Dean and Mae.

Dean shrugged. Mae gave him a quick look of reproof for his lack of conversational finesse and turned to their guest. "He seemed pleasant enough, if a bit too aware of his social consequence," she said with the frankness that was entirely characteristic of her, to the dismay of more than a few hapless souls who'd tried to condescend to her in the past.

Sharyn chuckled. "If you think *he's* aware of the family prominence, you should meet his mama. The mayor likes to pretend he's in charge around here, but everyone knows his mother is the one really running things. She calls him up, barks a few commands and suddenly he's got a new community project going. Usually at taxpayer expense. Margaret Peavy Vandover considers herself somewhat on a par with the queen mother."

"Why would the local citizens support a mayor who lets his mother tell him how to run the town?" Dean asked, bewildered by this glimpse of small-town politics.

"Habit," Sharyn admitted ruefully. "The Peavys have lived around here for years. Charles is the mayor, his cousin's chief of police and another cousin is a state senator. Not to mention the money the Peavys have poured into the town over the years. It has to be spent exactly the way they say, of course—and usually on something that carries the Peavy name, like the new Charles Peavy Memorial Library. Charles, Sr., was Margaret's father, and according to her, he fully qualifies for sainthood. He owned this inn once, by the way."

"The mayor said something about that," Mae acknowledged.

"Gaylon Peavy—Margaret's grandfather—married the widow of James Cameron, the British immigrant who built the inn back in the 1890s. Her name was . . . um . . . Amelia, I think. James died of influenza while she was expecting their twins. She married Gaylon about ten years later. She died five or six years after that. Gaylon took over the inn and operated it until his death in the thirties, after which Charles, his son from a previous marriage, took over. Charles sold it in the fifties."

"You know a great deal about the history of the inn," Dean commented, wondering why she hadn't told him much of this before. Perhaps because he'd never asked?

He'd taken one look at the place and had known he wanted it, whatever its history.

Sharyn smiled. "Everyone around here knows the story of the Cameron Inn. It's part of our local lore."

"Ah, yes. The ghosts," Mae said with satisfaction, getting to the part of the story that particularly interested her.

"Amelia's twins," Sharyn said, her eyes lighting up.

It was obvious that she, too, relished this part of the legend, Dean thought in resignation. Was he the only one around here who couldn't care less about silly old ghost stories? He'd outgrown them in his Boy Scout days.

As if sensing his disapproval, Sharyn threw a quick glance at Dean. "I *did* mention that the inn was supposed to be haunted," she reminded him. "You never seemed particularly interested, but I didn't want you to claim that I misrepresented the place when I sold it to you."

He nodded. "You did tell me. And, as you assumed, I wasn't particularly interested. I don't believe in ghosts."

How many more times, he wondered impatiently, was he going to have to say that before he could get on with the business of restoring and running his inn?

Mae dismissed her nephew with a wave of her hand. "*I'm* interested," she assured Sharyn. "I would love to hear about the ghosts who haunt my new home."

Sharyn hesitated a moment. "I wouldn't want to make you uncomfortable here . . ."

"Nonsense. I already love this old inn. I have from the moment Dean first showed it to me. I've sensed a, well, a welcoming presence from the old place since we first arrived. If there are ghosts," Mae said with a gentle smile, "I think they're pleased that someone is eager to restore their home to its former glory."

"From what I've been told, you're probably right. The twins supposedly loved this place wholeheartedly. Their mother was obsessed with the inn, which had been built by the first husband she'd adored, and she reportedly passed on her obsession for it to her children. They were so attached to it, it was rumored that the brother—Ian Cameron—was involved in bootlegging, maybe even murder, to make enough money to redecorate and enlarge the inn as soon as he was in charge."

Dean felt a chill breeze drift down the back of his shirt collar, much like that eerie cold he'd felt on the garden path. He shifted in his chair, telling himself he was being an idiot.

"Murder?" Mae repeated, looking properly shocked.

Sharyn nodded avidly. "Apparently, there was a big, very profitable bootlegging ring in this area, distributing booze to the gin joints and gambling houses that were operating in Hot Springs at that time. Hot Springs was quite a hotbed then, a favorite hangout for some notable historical figures, including organized crime bosses like Al Capone and Bugsy Siegel. Some thought Ian Cameron had become involved with those organizations. He'd made no secret that he planned to enlarge the inn as soon as he and his sister took over on their twenty-fifth birthday."

"Who was Ian supposed to have murdered?" Mae asked.

"A Prohibition officer from Little Rock. The officer was found dead only a mile from the inn. Two weeks later, Ian and Mary Anna were killed after being caught meeting with a bootlegger."

"And when was that?"

"February 14, 1921," Sharyn recited promptly. "Valentine's Day. Their twenty-fifth birthday."

"The day they were supposed to have taken over the inn?" Dean asked, following the story despite himself.

Sharyn nodded, obviously pleased that he was paying attention. "Their mother had left the inn to them in her will, naming their stepfather as executor of the estate until their twenty-fifth birthday. Some folks thought that the provision was his idea, that he persuaded her he had the inn's best interests at heart by making sure the twins were mature enough to run it successfully before turning it over to them. Maybe she thought she'd live longer than she did, and put the provision in her will to appease her second husband. But, anyway, he took over after she died and it's rumored that he and the twins had a lot of arguments about his management of the place. After they died, he automatically inherited the inn."

Dean cocked his head, thinking of all the murder mysteries he'd read. "Wasn't there any suspicion that Gaylon Peavy might have been responsible for the twins' deaths? After all, he conveniently inherited their inn..."

Sharyn shook her head. "Of course there were a few rumors to that effect—rumors Margaret and the mayor still take very personally—but it's highly unlikely. The twins were killed in a gun battle with a local police officer, a deputy named Tagert. He had been watching the place since the murder of the Prohibition officer, and he caught Ian and Mary Anna meeting with a known criminal, a man named Buck somebody."

She waved that point off with one hand. "Anyway, Ian and Buck reportedly opened fire, and Tagert shot back to defend himself. Tagert killed Buck. Mary Anna supposedly died in the crossfire. Some say Ian shot himself after he saw his sister fall. They were very close."

"How horrible," Mae murmured, her eyes dreamy as she seemed to be picturing the tragic scene.

Dean squirmed again in his chair, wondering if anyone else noticed how cold the room had become. Almost frigid.

He'd left instructions for the central-heating unit to be checked for safety reasons, but he suspected it would have to be replaced soon. Obviously it wasn't working properly.

Sharyn had turned back to face him. "You know the little shack at the back of your property? It was a caretaker's cottage. That's where the twins were meeting with Buck, the place where they died. Crates of booze were found there in the investigation that followed the shootings."

Dean's stomach tightened as he remembered that cold spot near the old shack. He visualized again the dark-haired woman on the path, looking at him so beseechingly. So . . . hauntedly.

A projection, he reminded himself curtly. What else could it have been? He wished to hell the culprit would present himself soon so Dean could put the incident out of his mind.

And still he heard himself asking, "You said people claim to have seen the twins here at the inn since their deaths?"

"Only a very few over the years," Sharyn admitted. "You know how these legends go—someone claims to know someone who claims to have seen them. Usually on Valentine's Day, of course, the day of their births and deaths. Of course, no one really even knows what they looked like. There are no surviving photographs of them. Some said Gaylon Peavy was so grief-stricken, he ordered all photos of his stepchildren destroyed."

"They died seventy-five years ago next month," Mae mused aloud. "Maybe Dean and I will see them, yet. Maybe they'll drift through the hallways at midnight on Valentine's Day or something equally dramatic."

Sharyn shivered visibly. "Don't even joke about that."

Mae laughed. "Unfortunately, I'm afraid I'm as prosaic as my nephew when it comes to ghosts. I don't really expect to see them, even though it might be an interesting experience."

"A terrifying experience, I would think," Sharyn said.

"I just hope no local jokesters decide to 'help' us see the ghosts on Valentine's Day," Dean muttered.

Both Sharyn and Mae looked confused by his words.

"What do you mean?" Sharyn asked. "No one around here would do anything like that. Oh, sure, there have been a few school kids who've done things over the years—boys trying to scare their girlfriends, practical jokers, you know the type. But it's unlikely something will happen to you."

"Whatever made you say that, Dean?" Mae asked, puzzled. "Has something already happened?"

He shook his head, uncertain why he was so reluctant to discuss the incident in the attic, and afterward on the garden path. "Forget it. It wouldn't work, anyway. I'd never fall for it."

Smiling, Mae glanced at Sharyn. In unison, they recited, "He doesn't believe in ghosts."

"I think he's made that clear enough," Sharyn added wryly as Mae laughed.

Sharyn didn't stay much longer, nor did Dean encourage her to. He walked her to the door, bade her a polite, if brief, good-night and locked the door behind her with a sense of relief that he and his aunt were finally alone again in their new home. He was tired, and he had a long day of manual labor ahead of him tomorrow. He wanted to turn in early.

"Good night, dear," Mae said a short while later, rising on tiptoe in the doorway to her bedroom to kiss her nephew's cheek.

"Good night, Aunt Mae. Sleep well."

She smiled. "Are you worried that the ghost stories over the dinner table will make me have nightmares? Or is it *your* dreams that concern you?"

He smiled chidingly. "Hardly. I'm too tired to dream tonight, anyway."

"Is that it?" she murmured, suddenly looking a bit sad. "Or have you simply forgotten how to dream, Dean?"

He frowned. "I don't know what you—"

She brushed off his words with a shake of her head. "Never mind. I'm just tired, myself. Good night."

She closed her door politely in his face.

Still a bit bewildered by her comment, Dean headed for his own bed. He really needed some sleep.

SOMETHING WOKE HIM in the middle of the night. Not quite a noise. Not quite a feeling. But something . . .

She was standing in the corner of his bedroom, among the shadows created by the soft glow of a night-light through the open bathroom doorway. She was still wearing the long white dress. And she still looked at him as though she desperately needed something from him.

Her lips moved. This time, he thought he heard her. Her voice was a soft, faint whisper, little more than a musical breeze.

"Lies," she said, the word shivering down his bare spine. "Everything she told you . . . lies. We didn't—it wasn't—oh, damnation."

Her form shimmered. Still groggy and disbelieving, Dean rubbed his eyes.

Her voice dropped even softer, a hint of sound at the very edge of his hearing. "Help us," she whispered with more than a touch of demand in the plea. "Please...help us . . ."

And she was gone.

Dean shook his head slowly, as though to clear it. Then he looked back at that now-unoccupied, shadow-filled corner.

A straight-backed chair sat there. The white shirt he'd worn earlier lay over it. *A dream*, he told himself.

He thought he knew what had happened. Despite his smugness with his aunt earlier, he had allowed his dreams to be influenced by Sharyn's fanciful stories. Still mostly asleep, he'd sat up in bed, spotted the white shirt and transformed it in his sleep-dazed mind into the beautiful woman he'd seen earlier.

Shaking his head in self-disgust, he fell back on the bed, staring at the ceiling with eyes now fully alert. What a first day he'd had here! He sincerely hoped it wasn't an omen.

He scowled. He believed in omens no more than he believed in ghosts. He refused to allow his new life to be marred by silly superstitions. Everyone dreamed.

Daylight would dawn, and life would go on. And soon this episode, like the others, would be forgotten.

But even as he closed his eyes and tried to force himself back to sleep, he thought he heard that soft, floating whisper. *"Please . . . help us."*

ANNA STAMPED her foot as she glared at the man lying in the bed, pretending to be asleep. He didn't hear her, just as he hadn't heard anything she'd been trying to say to him since he'd lain back down.

"Give it up, Anna. He doesn't even know you're here," her brother advised from her side.

She knew he was right, but it infuriated her that the man—Dean, she knew now—lay so close, yet so oblivious.

There had to be a reason he kept seeing her. She didn't know what it was, but she was becoming more certain each time she tried to contact him that this man was special.

No one else had ever seen them more than once, no one else had seemed so affected by their appearance— even though Dean wouldn't admit even to himself that he was seeing them. But she'd known from the first moment their eyes met that the key to her freedom was within this man's grasp.

She'd been there in the dining room, heard the horrible lies that woman . . . that bleached-blond scandalmonger . . . had told. She and Ian had heard the stories before, of course. Unseen, unheard, they had listened as others during the years had talked about the tragedy that had taken place here, reinforcing the lies that Stanley Tagert had apparently told that night.

Each time, Anna had reacted with fury and disbelief that no one had ever learned the truth. But tonight, hearing that woman telling her lies to Dean, Anna had been angrier than ever. Had she been able, she would have thrown the woman's peach cobbler right into her overpainted face.

Somehow, she had to reach Dean. She had to convince him that none of the tales were true. That she and Ian had been murdered and their reputations maligned for all the years since.

If Dean could help them, if he could find some way to clear their names, identify their killer, then they could be free. It made such sense to her, despite her brother's cynicism. It sounded exactly like something that would have happened in one of the novels Anna had so enjoyed reading in her youth.

If only she could make him understand.

Anna drifted closer to the bed, looking down at the bare-chested man beneath the covers. His eyes were closed, his breathing deep and even. He really was a very attractive man. His shoulders were broad, his chest solid, strong looking. He reminded her more of her brother than of her former fiancé, who had been fair-skinned and a bit soft. But Jeffrey had been very sweet and kind, she reminded herself quickly, feeling a little disloyal at her comparison. He would have made her an excellent husband.

That, too, had been denied her.

She reached out to the man in the bed. "Dean? Dean, can you hear me?"

Her fingertips brushed his face. An odd ripple of sensation went through her, reminding her of her childhood, when she and Ian had scuffed their shoes against the carpets and touched each other for the resulting static shock.

Dean frowned, brushed clumsily at his face, and rolled over onto his side without waking.

"He doesn't know you're here," Ian repeated gently. "We have to go, Anna."

She, too, felt the pull, the inexorable force that would take them away from the inn, to that silent, gray, empty place where they would drift with only each other for company until they could return again—whenever that might be.

She looked one last time at the man in the bed, wondering if he would still be here when she came back, or if he, too, would be part of the inn's history by then.

Somehow, she thought he'd be here.

3

A spirit, yet a woman too!
                    —William Wordsworth

TO DEAN'S RELIEF, he didn't see the ghostly woman
again during the next few days. Work began in earnest
on renovations, and the inn became a madhouse of ac-
tivity, with carpenters, plumbers, electricians and dec-
orators swarming through the place like hyperactive
ants.

Amazing, Dean thought cynically, how the promise
of a generous bonus could serve as an incentive for
quick and efficient work.

He was using every penny of his life savings on this
project. The financial risk he was taking would be
staggering if he allowed himself to dwell on it—which
he didn't. Even bankruptcy would be better than the
dull, grim, joyless routine he'd found himself living in
Chicago.

The townspeople welcomed him quite warmly, on
the whole. He was invited to join the chamber of com-
merce, the Rotarians, the Optimist Club, several local
churches, and was even scouted out as a potential coach
for Little League baseball, though he had to admit that
he hadn't had much experience with sports. Hunters
and fishermen inquired about his prowess with a gun
and a rod, but those sports had never appealed to him,
either.

When asked what he *did* enjoy doing in his leisure time, he was sorely stumped for an answer. Truth was, he'd never had much leisure time, having spent most of his adult life determinedly working his way up the corporate ladder.

He was good-naturedly teased about his northern accent and mannerisms, indicating that the local residents liked a good joke. Well enough to have concocted his ghostly visitor lady? Dean couldn't help wondering, though he still didn't understand why no one had yet claimed credit for the gag.

Fortunately, his maternal grandparents had lived twenty miles south of Atlanta and Dean had visited them often during his youth, so he wasn't totally ignorant of southern customs. He was a big fan of the "redneck" comedian, Jeff Foxworthy, and had been an avid Lewis Grizzard reader—he still mourned the loss of the late writer's laconic, blunt, often startlingly insightful humor—so Dean could hold his own with the local jokesters. He thought he was going to fit in just fine here once he'd had a chance to get to know everyone, and vice versa.

He met more people each time he went into town for supplies or on other errands. He found himself scanning faces, surreptitiously studying the shoppers at Groceries-4-Less and the discount store, the customers in line at the Bank of Destiny and the post office and diners in the local fast-food restaurants. So far, he hadn't caught a glimpse of a woman with dark hair, dark eyes and a face that had made his heart pound faster—and not from fear of ghosts.

Who *was* she? Would he ever see her again? He told himself he wondered only from mild curiosity. Certainly not for any more compelling reason.

He saw Mark Winter several times during that first week. Dean liked the dry-humored newspaper publisher, and thought it possible he'd made his first real friend in town. A good sign—if one believed in that sort of thing, of course.

On the first Sunday afternoon after arriving at the inn, Dean was kneeling on the front porch, pounding nails into a new board, when his aunt appeared in the doorway, her red hair humorously askew, her face liberally smudged with dust. "Dean, you have a telephone call. It's Bailey."

Setting his hammer aside, Dean climbed to his feet, grinning at his aunt's appearance. "What have you been doing, Aunt Mae? Wrestling dust bunnies?"

She smiled. "I was in the attic when the telephone rang."

He almost stumbled on his way to the front door. His grin quickly disappeared. "The—er—attic? Why?"

"Just curiosity," she answered, apparently surprised by the sharpness of his tone. "Is there some reason I shouldn't go up there?"

"No," Dean said after only a momentary pause. "No reason. Just, um, be careful on the stairs, okay?"

"Of course." Mae looked at him a bit oddly as he picked up the telephone in the lobby, but then left him in privacy to take his call.

Dean's younger sister, Bailey, was an antiques dealer in Chicago. "Dean, you'll never believe it," she said with characteristic enthusiasm. "I've found a fantastic buy on a turn-of-the-century sitting-room set for your inn. Sofa, love seat, two wing-back chairs and a footstool. It will be great for the honeymoon suite we discussed. All you need to add are a couple of tables and a lamp, and the room's done."

"Sounds great, Bailey. Thanks."

"I'm still looking for bedroom pieces. Got my eye on a 1914 twin-bed set with a matching bureau and a 1926 full-size maple bed with a triple dresser and a matching nightstand."

"Whatever you can get," he replied, having already discussed his needs and his budget with her.

"So, how's it going? Aunt Mae said the renovations are well under way."

"There's a lot to be done, of course, but we've made a good start. I hope to be able to open for business sometime around the first of July."

"Whew! You're really pushing it, aren't you? Considering how much you said had to be done."

"Yeah," he admitted ruefully. "We're practically tearing out some walls and building new ones. But I'd like to cash in on at least the latter part of the summer tourist season, and be well established by the time horse-racing season begins in Hot Springs in February."

"Then I'd better get busy filling your bedrooms, hadn't I?"

He smiled at her matter-of-fact tone and agreed.

They chatted for a few more minutes. Sensing that something was troubling his sister, Dean asked if anything was wrong.

"Oh, no," she assured him with an airiness that made him even more concerned. "I'm just tired, I guess. We've been pretty busy at the shop."

"How's the new romance coming along?"

There was a notable pause before she answered. "I really couldn't say."

Dean shook his head.

His sister *would* persist in getting involved with guys with emotional problems. She'd earned herself the reputation of "Miss Lonely Hearts" because of her inability to turn away anyone she felt needed her. Dean had been warning her for years that someday she was going to realize that she'd taken care of everyone's needs except her own—and she would regret it.

Unwilling to intrude on her personal life, he kept silent. If she wanted to tell him about her problems, she would, in her own time.

Bailey changed the subject by bringing up the ghosts. "Aunt Mae told me all about them," she said. "If I were you, I'd do some research and find out as much about the legend as possible. Your guests will probably want to know all the details."

He sighed. "I keep telling everyone, I have no intention of capitalizing on old ghost stories. I'm running an inn, not a haunted lodge."

"Dean, it was the age and the history of the inn that appealed to you in the first place. Don't you want to know all the details, even the legends connected to it?"

He couldn't argue with that, though he might have liked to try. "Well, when you put it that way..."

"I'm sure the local library or newspaper office would be able to help you print up a brief history of the inn. You really should consider it. Your guests would probably enjoy it."

"I'll consider it."

"Great. I can't wait to come and see the place again." She had seen the inn only once, when Dean was considering whether or not to buy the place and had flown her down to ask her opinion. Like Dean, Bailey had fallen in love with it at first sight, and her encouragement had strongly influenced his decision.

"I hope you'll be able to come soon," he told her affectionately. "I miss you already."

"Oh, by the way," Bailey said just as he was about to hang up. "I ran into Gloria yesterday."

He brought the receiver reluctantly back to his ear. "Did you?"

"Mmm. She was still trying to pump me for information about your emotional health. The conceited bi— Well, anyway, she's absolutely convinced that you're pining away for her and have suffered an emotional breakdown as a result."

"She's wrong." Dean's words were curt.

"I know that. She just can't stand to think that you're better off without her. Which you are. Much. As I said in so many words to her."

Dean winced. "I'm sure you did." Bailey shared their aunt's sometimes ill-timed bluntness.

"She really hates me," Bailey said cheerfully. "But I can live with it. Bye, Dean. Talk to you soon."

Dean hung up the phone, then stood for a moment leaning against the reception desk, tugging absently at his lower lip. His thoughts were jumbled, ranging from concerns about his sister's happiness to worrying about whether he really could have all the renovations finished in time to open the inn by July.

His eyes were focused blankly on one corner of the empty lobby, and he was dimly aware of the sound of hammering and pounding from somewhere on the second story above him, where the carpenters and electricians were working that afternoon. He'd have to go up soon and check on their progress. Later, he had an appointment with a decorator and a . . .

He frowned, his planning coming to an abrupt halt. Something was odd about the corner he was staring at.

The wall seemed to be shimmering, going hazy, as though a film had come over his eyes.

He blinked, closed his eyes and rubbed them, then opened them again. The haze was even thicker now. White. When he squinted, he could almost make out a pale face with pleading dark eyes . . .

"Dean? Dean, look what I found! You'll never believe it."

At the sound of his aunt's voice, Dean snapped his head around. "In here, Aunt Mae."

When he looked back at the corner, the apparition—or whatever it had been—was gone.

The walls looked normal. Grimy, cracked, faded, but normal. No face. No pleading eyes.

"I am *not* having a breakdown," Dean muttered with a ferocious glare, as though confronting his ex-wife.

"Goodness, what a frown," Mae exclaimed, bustling through the doorway from the hall. "Stop glowering, Dean, and look at what I found in the attic."

With one last scowl at the offending corner, Dean turned to his aunt, who looked even more disheveled than before.

"What is it?" he asked, noting that she held a length of half-rotted fabric in her left hand and what might have been a small wooden picture frame in her right. He wrinkled his nose when he caught a whiff of a musty, mildewy smell emanating from the fabric.

"I found a box of old fabrics and pieces of clothing," she explained, waving the dark-colored scrap enthusiastically, making Dean sneeze when dust flew from it. "I thought we could use them for our decorating. Not these pieces, of course," she added quickly when he would have spoken. "But maybe the colors and prints will give us ideas."

He looked doubtful. Judging from the scrap in her hand, he wasn't sure he could even tell what color it had once been, much less make out the pattern.

"But this is what I really wanted to show you," Mae said, holding out the frame and looking expectant. "Who do you suppose this is?"

Dean took the frame without much enthusiasm, still partially preoccupied with his former concerns—and trying not to dwell on that odd sensation he'd just experienced. He glanced down at the black-and-white photograph, and noted that it was old, and faded, and that the two subjects, a man and a woman, had been posed in front of the inn.

Guessing that the photo had been taken sometime around 1920, he ignored the people and studied the inn with a proprietary eye, examining the changes and additions that had been made since that time. He wondered if there were any other such photographs of the place that he could use for reference in his renovations.

And then something made him look more closely at the couple in the picture. His knees gave way, and he sagged against the counter, his gaze riveted on the face of the woman.

It was *her*. The woman he'd seen in the attic, and on the garden path. And again in his own bedroom.

There was no way he could be mistaken about that face.

She was, quite simply, gorgeous. Her glossy, dark hair was shaped into a soft upsweep that framed her delicate, fair-skinned face. Dark, expressive eyes. Perfectly formed nose. A chin that hinted of willfulness. Her mouth was a perfect bow, lips slightly parted.

Even in the faded, monochromatic photograph, he could sense her sparkle, her vitality. Her eyes gleamed with a real, lifelike twinkle.

Just the way they'd looked when he'd seen her three times before.

"Dean?" Mae asked, moving quickly toward him.

Though he heard her, he couldn't seem to respond to his aunt. All his concentration was still centered on the photograph.

Reluctantly, he dragged his gaze from the woman in the picture and looked at her brother.

Brother? He frowned, wondering where that thought had come from. For all he knew, they could have been husband and wife. But, no. They looked too much alike. Eerily alike. Brother and sister, he would bet on it.

Twins, most likely.

Dean studied the young man's somber, rather piercing dark eyes, straight nose, lean cheeks and firm, strong chin. There was a hint of a temper in the rather arrogant set of his head.

A few generations earlier, he might have been an Old West outlaw, or a cool, daring lawman. In modern times, he could be a valued member of an organized-crime family—or a maverick cop. He had that dangerous look that indicated either a complete disregard for the law or a grim determination to make sure others adhered to it.

Bootlegger. Murderer. Thinking of the tale Sharyn had told, Dean wondered now if it had all been true.

"Dean?" Mae repeated, placing a hand on his arm. "Are you all right? You've gone pale."

"I—er—sorry, I got distracted," he managed to say, still looking at the photograph.

"It's them, isn't it? I've found the only photo of the twins," Mae said. "I thought it was, but I wanted to see if you agreed."

"It certainly could be the Cameron twins," Dean admitted. *How could he have seen her? Had the woman he'd seen been an uncannily similar-looking descendant of Mary Anna Cameron?* Or—

He swallowed.

"Dean, are you sure you're feeling well? You really don't look so good," Mae fretted.

For just a moment, he considered telling her. About the first sighting in the attic. The cold feeling on the pathway, followed by his second encounter with the figure, and his conclusion that he'd been the victim of a joke. The woman's whispered plea in the middle of the night in his bedroom.

He rejected the impulse almost immediately. This wasn't something he could talk about. Not yet, anyway. "I'm fine, Aunt Mae. I'd better get upstairs and check on the carpenters."

He handed the photograph back to her with a reluctance he didn't quite understand. He was aware that his aunt was watching him with a mixture of bewilderment and concern as he abruptly left the room.

DEAN HARDLY TOUCHED his dinner that evening. Too restless to read or watch television, and knowing he would never get to sleep if he tried turning in early, he made his excuses to his aunt and went into the garden, where he paced, muttered and tried to figure out what the hell had been happening to him.

He still hadn't completely abandoned the possibility that he'd been the victim of a joke. Even if the photograph really *was* of the Cameron twins—and he had every reason to assume that it was—that didn't mean the long-dead Mary Anna Cameron had been popping out of her spectral plane, or whatever, to visit him. He lived in an age of computer-generated magic, a decade when movie actors could play scenes with dead historical figures, when special effects had to be pretty damned amazing to be truly special.

But would anyone in tiny Destiny, Arkansas, be skilled enough to bring to life a seventy-five-year-old photograph? And if so, why pull such a complicated hoax on Dean without at least taking credit for the stunt?

He turned to pace in the other direction, away from the inn this time. It was a cold night, and he burrowed into his leather jacket, his hands deep in the pockets. His cheeks were chilled, his nose a bit numb and his breath hung in ghostly little clouds ahead of him, eerily illuminated by the three-quarter moon overhead. He ignored the minor discomforts, still too restless to go back inside. Unwilling to face his aunt's worriedly questioning eyes.

He wanted to be alone.

But, suddenly, he wasn't.

"Hell," he muttered when the woman stood in front of him on the path, primly smoothing her long white skirts.

She cocked an eyebrow. "A gentleman doesn't curse in front of a lady," she commented, and though her voice sounded a bit muffled, as though coming from farther away than she appeared, he could hear her quite clearly this time.

"Oh, this is great," he grumbled. "Now I'm getting chewed out by my hallucinations."

She laughed, the sound distant, musical. Like wind chimes heard from a neighbor's lawn. She looked up and to her right, as though talking to someone standing beside her. "He still thinks he's hallucinating," she said. "But at least he hears me this time. I *told* you I could do it if I tried hard enough!"

Dean frowned gloomily. Terrific. Even his hallucination was hallucinating. As far as he could see, she was talking to a scraggly cedar tree.

The woman suddenly looked startled. "What?" she asked the tree. "But—why?"

Dean waited politely for the tree to reply. He wouldn't have been entirely surprised had it done so, the way things were going tonight. But apparently the woman heard something he didn't.

She turned to face him again, her dark eyes wide with curiosity. "You *do* see me, don't you?" she demanded.

Dean shrugged. "Oh, what the hell. Sure, I see you. Want to tell me how you're doing this?"

She ignored his question and motioned to the empty space beside her. "And Ian? Do you see him, as well?"

"Ian, is it?" Dean shook his head. Whoever was behind this was a stickler for details. "Is he, by chance, a pooka?"

She looked puzzled. "A what?"

"A pooka. Like Harvey, Jimmy Stewart's bunny friend."

She placed her hands on her hips, studying him in frank bewilderment. "I haven't the faintest idea what you're talking about."

"Fictional characters," he explained. "Imaginary creatures. Like invisible rabbits. Leprechauns. Santa Claus. Ghosts," he added grimly.

She dismissed the pooka question with an impatient wave of one slender hand. "I wish you'd answer me. Do you see Ian or not?"

"Not," he answered, his tone flat. "I see only you. Now, I'm giving you three seconds to tell me what's going on here or to get the hell off my property before I call the police."

"How very interesting," she murmured, seeming unintimidated by his threat. "I wonder why you see only one of us?"

Forcing himself to study her objectively, Dean noticed that she appeared more solid this time than she had before. Though she still looked somewhat ethereal, he couldn't see through her. As far as he could tell, she was no projection, but a real woman. An incredibly beautiful woman.

A woman who could have stepped directly out of that old photograph his aunt had found in the attic.

He moved a step closer. "Who are you?"

"My name is Mary Anna Cameron," she said, holding her ground.

"Bull."

Her delicate eyebrows drew downward. "You really shouldn't talk that way," she scolded. "It isn't proper."

"Neither is pretending to be a ghost," he retorted, wondering how quickly she'd duck away if he reached for her. Very slowly, he began to ease his hands out of his pockets. "Did you think it would be funny to see me scream and run? If so, I'm sorry you were disappointed."

She shook her head. "I didn't expect you to scream. Ian expected you to, but I told him, from what I've seen of you, I didn't believe you'd be such a coward."

"And have you seen much of me?" he asked mockingly.

He would have sworn her cheeks darkened in the pale moonlight. Even further proof, of course, that she wasn't who she claimed to be. He doubted that ghosts, if they existed, would blush.

"Ian has been trying to keep me out of your private rooms, but I wanted to talk to you," she explained, sounding apologetic. "It was only by accident that I saw you unclothed earlier this evening. I turned away, and I really didn't see anything more than that cute little heart-shaped birthmark on your—er—"

She winced as she turned toward the cedar tree. "But he asked," she said. "I was just trying to explain... You don't think he meant . . . ? Oh."

She looked contritely back at Dean. "Ian has always said I talk too much when I'm nervous."

How the *hell* had she known about that embarrassing birthmark? He'd spent most of his life trying to hide the thing from all but a very select few.

He'd had all he could take. His temper was slow to ignite, but when it did, it flamed. He reached out and took hold of her bare arm, just beneath the fluttery little sleeve of her floaty white dress.

And then he froze.

The woman who called herself Mary Anna Cameron might have looked real enough, but Dean knew from the moment he touched her that his entire world, every belief he'd ever held, had just been irrevocably changed.

4

True Love is Like Ghosts,
Which everybody talks about
and few have seen.
                    —François, Duc de la Rochefoucauld

IT WAS LIKE holding a woman made of marble. Her skin was unnaturally cool and smooth. There was no friction when he moved his fingers, no warmth, no...life.

She had gone very still, watching him with wide, wary eyes. Because he couldn't resist, Dean lifted his free hand to touch her face.

She didn't flinch when he stroked her cheek—her ice-cold cheek—or when he slid his fingers down to the hollow in her throat, where her pulse should have throbbed.

He felt nothing.

Their gazes locked. Dean couldn't have spoken, even if he'd known what to say.

It was almost a shock to hear her voice again. She wasn't speaking to Dean. "No, Ian, it's all right," she said, her tone soothing. "Just give us a minute."

Somehow, Dean managed to speak. "What *are* you?" he asked hoarsely.

"I told you," she said in that same, soothing voice. "I'm Mary Anna Cameron."

"Mary Anna Cameron died seventy-five years ago."

Her expressive dark eyes turned sad. "Yes."

"Then you're . . ."

She wrinkled her nose in distaste. "I suppose one could call me a ghost."

"I don't . . ." His words trailed away.

". . .believe in ghosts," she finished for him. "I know. You've said so often enough. But as you see—and feel— I'm here. It's very odd. No one's been able to touch me before, though a very few have seen us."

Us. He looked cautiously around, but still saw nothing more than that scraggly cedar tree. "Your brother is here?"

"Yes." She nodded toward an apparently empty space beside her. "Right there."

"Why can't I see him?"

"We don't know." She looked genuinely perplexed. "It doesn't make sense to us, either."

"This is crazy," Dean muttered, shaking his head.

She brushed that useless observation aside. "Dean, we think you can help us. Or at least, *I* think so. Ian isn't so sure."

"Help you? What do you mean?"

"We—*I* think we're here because of those wicked lies that were told about us. None of the things that woman said about us is true. Ian wasn't a bootlegger and he is certainly no murderer. We didn't die in a shoot-out with Stanley Tagert. Tagert lied."

"Even if what you say is true, what do you want *me* to do about it?"

She continued to hold his gaze with her own. "Prove it."

He snorted. "Yeah. Right."

"I'm serious. You must do this for us. You're the only one who can. The only one we—I can talk to. The only one to hear our side of the story. You have to help us prove our innocence."

"I wouldn't know how to begin. And, besides," he added lamely, still trying to deal with his shaken beliefs, "I'm very busy now. I have my own life to live."

Anger kindled in her lovely eyes. "At least you *have* a life," she snapped. "We . . . oh, damnation."

One moment he was holding her arm. The next moment . . . he wasn't.

She was a few feet away from him now. As he watched, she grew fainter. Translucent. She seemed to shimmer in the shadows, as though illuminated by a faint glow from within her. Her voice sounded far away. "Dean. You must help us. You're the only one who can."

"Wait," he said, instinctively moving toward her. "I—"

But she was gone. "Hell," Dean muttered, closing his eyes and rubbing them wearily. His heart was pounding, his skin damp and his mind a whirl of doubt and wonder.

Maybe his ex-wife was right.

Maybe he *was* losing his mind.

THE OFFICES of the *Destiny Daily* were somewhat less than luxurious. In fact, Dean decided, looking around, they were downright shabby.

The building itself looked at least fifty years old, and Dean wouldn't have been surprised to hear that it had been that long since the lobby had been painted. Whatever color the walls had once been, they were now a grubby grayish-brown. So were the windows.

A battered reception desk sat in the center of the room, with a row of metal filing cabinets leaning drunkenly behind it. A computer monitor and telephone were on the desk, almost buried beneath messy stacks of papers. The telephone was ringing and had been since Dean had entered. No one rushed to answer it.

A chipped fake-wood credenza held a fax machine, computer printer, several overflowing wire baskets and stacks of photographs and newspapers. Other than the clutter, Dean saw no evidence of human habitation, though he heard noises coming from somewhere at the back.

He'd just decided to go looking for someone, when Mark Winter strolled through a doorway. His sandy eyebrows lifted in surprise when he saw Dean. "Oh. Hi, Dean. What can I do for you?"

Dean motioned toward the still patiently ringing phone. "Er, shouldn't someone answer that?"

"Oh. Yeah, I guess so. Hang on a minute." Mark scooped up the receiver and held it to his ear. "*Destiny Daily.*"

The call didn't take long. Dean didn't bother to eavesdrop. He used the time to try to decide how best to explain his purpose in being here. It wasn't easy, considering he didn't exactly know, himself, why he'd decided to look into the deaths of the Cameron twins. To satisfy his own curiosity, if for no other reason.

Mark looked at Dean closely when he concluded the call. "Everything going okay out at the inn, Dean? Excuse me for saying so, but you look like hell."

Dean cleared his throat and shoved a hand through his hair, wishing the deceptively lazy-mannered journalist wasn't quite so perceptive.

"Yeah, everything's fine," he said with a casual shrug. "Just didn't get much sleep last night."

"The ghosts keeping you awake rattling chains or something?"

Dean managed a smile. "Something like that. And speaking of the ghosts . . ."

Mark looked startled. "You haven't really seen them, have you? I was only joking."

"Actually, I'm interested in doing some research on them," Dean explained, neatly avoiding the question. "My sister has convinced me that I should know the full history of the inn, just in case any of my guests inquire. I thought you could lead me in the right direction to start my research. Old newspapers, perhaps?"

Mark looked indecisive for a moment, as though there was something he wanted to say, but wasn't sure he should. "I have a few things that might be helpful to you," he said finally.

"What?"

"Actually, I've done some research, myself," Mark confessed a bit sheepishly. "A couple of years ago, when I first moved here and heard the legend, I thought it might make an interesting book."

"You're writing a book?" Dean asked, startled.

Mark grimaced. "Nah. It's just a bug I get every so often. The urge generally leaves me after I sweat blood over the first few pages."

"And you thought of writing a book about the Cameron Inn?"

He nodded. "Seemed like a good idea at the time. And then . . . well, things started happening when I looked into the twins' deaths." He finished the sentence in a mumble.

Dean cocked his head, studying Mark closely. "What things?"

Had Mark, perhaps, encountered a beautiful, ghostly woman who begged him to clear her brother's name? Had he, too, become obsessed with that vision, losing sleep, losing interest in food, unable to concentrate on anything else? Had he wondered when he would see her again? Or what might have happened between them, if she'd been real?

Had Mark thought *he* was losing his mind?

"Nothing supernatural," Mark said with a quick laugh, as though sensing the direction Dean's thoughts had taken. "Just weird stuff I probably caused myself, maybe because I wasn't committed enough to the idea of actually finishing a book. You know, notes disappeared, sources suddenly dried up, people stopped talking. Maybe if I'd pursued it more seriously, I'd have figured out what went wrong. But then the financial situation here at the paper turned critical and I was too busy saving my livelihood to think about legends."

Surreptitiously, Dean glanced around the shabby lobby. Was the newspaper still in desperate straits?

Again, Mark seemed to read his thoughts. "Things are better now, though obviously I'm never going to get rich running a small-town daily. But it's a good life. Helluva lot better than the rat race of political reporting."

"That's your background?"

"Yeah. Let's just say I burned out. The *Destiny Daily* became a comfortable refuge at a time when I badly needed one."

"You said things got weird when you started looking into the twins' deaths. Was there any evidence that someone was trying to keep you from finding out the truth?" Dean phrased the question carefully, since he didn't want to go into too much detail about his own interest in the story.

Mark frowned. "I was just beginning to wonder about that, myself, when everything started going to hell here at the paper. After that, there wasn't time to think about it. And then, once I had the situation here under control, I guess I just forgot about it."

"You don't suppose your problems at the paper were connected, do you? A way of getting your attention off the Cameron twins and back onto your own business?"

Mark went still, his gaze sharpening. "Damn," he muttered. "I must really be losing my edge. Covering elementary-school talent programs has dulled my once-suspicious, cynical nature."

"Then it *is* possible?"

"It's something I should have thought about," Mark admitted. "But—"

He went silent for a moment, thoughtfully stroking his chin, and then he shook his head. "It isn't likely, Dean. For one thing, why would anyone care about a seventy-five-year-old scandal? It makes a nice, spooky little legend, but it hardly affects anyone's life these days."

"What about the Peavy family? The twins' stepfather inherited the inn when they died. I'm assuming the family's current prominence in the community began then."

"Not exactly," Mark corrected. "The stepfather, Gaylon Peavy, was never overly successful with the inn. After his death, his son, Charles—the mayor's grandfather—took over and kept it running until he could find a buyer, but the family money came from shrewd investments Charles made after selling the inn."

"Investments in what?"

Mark started to answer, then stopped and shrugged. "I'm not sure, exactly. Everyone just said Charles Peavy was a smart investor."

"We can still assume that his initial investment capital came from the sale of the inn. Which his father conveniently inherited when the twins died in the mysterious shoot-out."

Mark cocked his head. "You have reason to believe Gaylon Peavy was involved in the twins' deaths? Have you found something at the inn? What—a journal? A diary?"

Dean shook his head. "Nothing like that. It's just that the story as it's been told to me doesn't quite ring true. Something's off—or maybe I've just read too many murder mysteries," he finished self-deprecatingly.

Mark didn't smile. "I'm a fan of the genre, myself."

"Maybe we've *both* read too many."

Mark seemed to come to a sudden decision. "Tell you what. I'll let you look over my notes and I'll make the old newspaper files available to you whenever you want to go through them. I'll also give you some names that might be helpful to you. In return, I'd appreciate your telling me if you find out anything interesting. There could be a book in this, after all. At the very least, a newspaper article."

Dean wasn't at all sure he wanted his inn used as the setting for a ghost book, but he felt he owed Mark something. "If I find anything conclusive, I'll discuss it with you," he said.

Mark chuckled. "Very carefully phrased. I like you, Gates."

Dean smiled. "I'd better get back to the inn. God only knows what my aunt and the decorator will come up with if I don't keep an eye on them."

"I'll drop my notes by the inn as soon as I get a chance."

"Anytime. Thanks, Mark."

"Yeah, sure. This could get interesting."

Dean wondered what the other man would say if he knew just how interesting the situation had already become.

DEAN WAS LEANING over a table in the inn lobby, trying to feign interest in the scraps of fabric and wallpaper littering the table's surface. His aunt crowded close to his left side, paying avid attention as the decorator droned on about options and possibilities.

"Or we could go with the cabbage-rose print and the pastel plaid for accent pieces. Maybe a touch of saffron," the painfully thin, dramatically coiffed woman suggested with smug appreciation for her own cleverness.

"Oh, no, not saffron. Ian *detests* yellow."

The feminine voice came from very close to Dean's right ear, so close that he jumped, scattering samples everywhere. He whirled, bumping the table and dislodging even more samples.

Mary Anna Cameron was standing less than three feet away, looking at him with a mischievous smile.

"This is getting much easier," she commented. "Contacting you, I mean."

Dean couldn't believe she had made her appearance this time in front of witnesses. "What are you—"

"Dean?" His aunt rested a hand on his arm. "Dear, what is it? What's wrong?"

He didn't take his eyes from Mary Anna, who waited politely for him to reply. "She's—"

"Mr. Gates, if you don't care for the saffron, we could select an alternate color." The decorator sounded annoyed.

Dean was amazed that the women weren't screaming in shock—gasping in surprise, at the very least. After all, a ghost had just materialized right in front of them.

"Aunt Mae, surely you see . . ." His voice faded.

"I don't think they can see me, Dean," Mary Anna said.

"I'm not very fond of the saffron, either. I'm sure Ms. Buchanan can come up with a color scheme we both like better," his aunt assured him, patting his arm. "Let's talk about it, shall we?"

Mary Anna was looking at the table, her nose wrinkled in distaste. "Cabbage roses are so common. Isn't there anything more original available?"

"I can't do this now," he told her through clenched teeth. "Can't you see I'm busy?"

"But, Dean, you're the one who set up this meeting for today," his aunt protested.

The decorator lifted her pointed nose in apparent affront. "I, too, have a very busy schedule, Mr. Gates. If this wasn't a convenient time for you, you should have let me know earlier."

"But—"

"The workmen are all gone for the afternoon, Dean. What is it you have to do now?"

He looked at his aunt. "I—"

"I rather like the one with the birds and vines," Mary Anna mused, reclaiming his attention. "Instead of yellow, you could use dark red as an accent, though your decorator will probably call it something fancier, like vermilion."

How could they not see her? Hear her? She looked so damned real. So . . . alive.

He was pretty sure he could touch her again if he tried. He shoved his hands into his pockets.

"I'm, er, sorry," he said to the decorator and his aunt, though he kept his gaze on Mary Anna. "I was thinking about something else."

"So you *do* want to continue?" Ms. Buchanan looked torn between walking out in a huff and staying to collect her sizable fee.

"Uh, yeah, sure." He stabbed a finger at the table, trying to look interested. "How about that paper there? The one with the birds and vines? And maybe we could use some red with it? I, uh, I like red."

Mary Anna smiled in satisfaction.

Ms. Buchanan pursed her thin mouth. "That *is* a possibility, I suppose."

"No yellow," Mary Anna said.

"No yellow," Dean repeated obediently.

"No yellow," Ms. Buchanan agreed with a sigh.

Mary Anna looked quite pleased with herself.

"As for the front sitting room," Ms. Buchanan began, clearly trying to salvage her expert control of the meeting. "I was thinking perhaps hunter-green walls with bright white trim and paisley rugs. We'll have to get rid of that dark wood paneling and heavy crown molding, of course."

Mary Anna gasped. "Over my dead...er...well, you know. Don't let her touch my father's walls or molding, Dean. My mother said he loved that wood!"

"We're not tearing out the paneling," Dean said in resignation. "Or the crown molding."

Ms. Buchanan looked seriously irked at having her judgment questioned so often. "And just what is *your* preference, Mr. Gates?" she asked, her tone chilly enough to frost grapes.

Dean looked ironically at Mary Anna. "I'm sure I'll come up with something."

Mary Anna smiled. "Do you think this will take much longer? I'd like to speak to you, in private."

He lifted an eyebrow. "Must it be now?"

"No, Dean, of course we don't have to make any final decisions now," Mae said before Mary Anna could answer. "But we should decide soon so Ms. Buchanan can place the order."

"I, uh, sorry, Aunt Mae, what did you say?"

"You really are out of it," she scolded, peering at him through her glittery red glasses. "Maybe we should call it a day and let you get some rest. I think you've given Ms. Buchanan a clearer idea of your taste now. Perhaps next time we meet, she'll have some new drawings and samples to show us."

"Why do you need her, anyway?" Mary Anna asked curiously. "Anyone can choose paint and wallpaper. It's not really all that difficult. And if you're trying to put everything back the way it was, I can tell you exactly what it looked like when my mother last decorated it."

Dean attempted to ignore the helpful ghost as he ushered Ms. Buchanan out of the inn with more haste than grace.

"Dean, whatever is the matter with you?" his aunt asked in exasperation, her hands on her ample hips. "You were quite rude to Ms. Buchanan. She may never come back now."

"I didn't like her, anyway," Mary Anna piped in. "She seemed awfully high in the instep to me. Who does she think she is, coming in here and trying to vandalize my inn?"

Dean glared at her. "Might I remind you that it's *my* inn?"

Mae's chin quivered. "I'm well aware of that, Dean. I was only trying to . . ."

Now he really felt like a heel. He placed an arm around his aunt's plump shoulders and gave the ghost a look of reproof.

"Aunt Mae, I'm sorry," he said. "Please don't be upset. I'm afraid I'm not myself today. I got very little sleep last night and it's made me surly."

Mae's attitude changed immediately from hurt to solicitous. "You aren't coming down with anything, are you, dear?" she asked, placing a hand against his forehead, the way she had when he was just a boy. "You do feel warm. Maybe we should call a doctor."

Feeling even worse about his behavior, Dean hugged her. "I don't need a doctor," he assured her. "Maybe I'll just go to my room and lie down for a while. I'm sure I'll be fine after a couple of hours' rest."

"That's very good," Mary Anna said approvingly. "I'll meet you in your room." As he watched, she vanished.

Dean lingered a few minutes making sure his aunt was fully mollified, assuring her again that there was really no need to summon a doctor, agreeing that yes, chicken soup would probably be a good thing to have for dinner.

And then he headed for his bedroom, grimly determined to have a long talk with a bothersome, much-too-beautiful ghost.

ANNA WAS WAITING when Dean stormed into his bedroom. She was sitting on the bed, her skirts folded neatly around her, and noted in amusement that he looked furious.

His anger didn't bother her. She'd had enough experience with Ian not to be easily intimidated by a man's temper. In fact, she was rather pleased that she'd managed to make Dean lose his.

He would have a hard time denying her existence if she had the ability to infuriate him.

"I thought that woman would never leave," she commented.

He narrowed his eyes. His voice was very quiet, but his tone was that of a man accustomed to having his orders obeyed. "Don't ever do that to me again."

Anna had never cared for being at the receiving end of orders—as those who'd once known her could have told him. She cocked her head and smiled, her expression faintly challenging. "And just how do you plan to stop me?" she asked a bit too politely.

He hesitated. And then, since there wasn't really anything he could say, he ignored the question. "What did you want to talk to me about?" he asked instead.

Satisfied that she'd made her point, Anna smiled once more. "I wanted to ask if you've made any progress in finding out the truth about what happened to Ian and me."

Dean scowled again. She wished he would smile back at her. She'd seen him smile at his aunt, and had been struck by how it had transformed his face from ordinarily pleasant to heart-flutteringly attractive. She had a sudden, foolish urge to have him smile at *her* that way.

"It was only yesterday that you asked me to look into it," he said, still frowning. "I haven't had time to find out anything yet, even if there's anything for me to discover."

"Was it only yesterday?" She winced. "Sorry. I tend to lose track of time. It seems like longer to me."

"Just, uh, where do you go when I can't see you?" Dean asked curiously, taking a cautious step closer to the bed. "I mean, do you just sort of hang around, watching us?"

She wrinkled her nose. The new direction the conversation had taken made her uncomfortable. She didn't like to think of herself as a ghost, when she felt so little different from the way she'd been before.

"Of course not. Oh, sometimes we can 'hang around,' as you call it, watching. But most of the time, we're . . . somewhere else. A place that's gray and cold and strange, where there's no one but each other to talk to. Ian says it feels like a waiting room, in a way. We've always known it was only temporary. I think we'll leave there—and here—once you've cleared our names, and proven once and for all that we were not criminals."

"Is Ian here now?" Dean asked, looking suspiciously around his bedroom, ignoring—deliberately, she suspected—her confidence in his eventual success at solving the mystery.

She shook her head. "He's there. Waiting for me."

At first, Anna had been surprised to learn that it was becoming easier for her to return to the inn at will. And then she'd discovered that she could do so even without Ian's company.

She'd persuaded him to stay behind this time, telling him that his presence distracted her when she was concentrating on talking to Dean. After all, she'd added with a laugh, it wasn't as though her brother had to protect her virtue. What could happen between a living innkeeper and a ghost?

Ian hadn't shared her amusement.

"How long can you stay?" Dean asked.

"I don't know," she admitted. "It's different every time."

Dean sat warily on the edge of the bed beside her, close enough to touch her if he reached out, which he didn't.

"Mary Anna," he began.

"Anna," she corrected with a smile. "My friends call me Anna."

"Anna," he repeated huskily, his gaze locked with hers. "You really are beautiful." The words seemed to startle him, as though he hadn't intended to say them aloud.

Anna felt something warm blossom inside her, the first real warmth she'd felt in longer than she could remember. Her smile trembled, then deepened. "Thank you. It's been...a very long time since I've heard that."

She was suddenly struck by the oddity of their situation. She was having a conversation with a good-looking man who'd been born years after her. A *living* man.

It was pointless for her to flirt with him, or to be so senselessly flattered by his compliment. And there was nothing to be gained by wasting time imagining what it would be like to be held in those strong arms, clasped against his broad, solid-looking chest.

She needed him, but only because there was a chance that he could help her and Ian escape the gray loneliness of the prison that had held them for the past seventy-five years. There could be no other bond between her and Dean Gates.

"You didn't have a chance to find out *anything* about us today?" she asked, deliberately returning her thoughts to the favor she'd asked of him.

"No."

She knew he must see the disappointment on her face. He quickly added, "But I did ask some questions at the newspaper office. The editor said he would help me with my research."

She was delighted, as pleased that he'd bothered to ask as by the results. He *was* going to help her! "Dean, that's wonderful! When can you start?"

He held up a hand. "Hey, don't rush me, all right? I've got a lot going on right now with these renovations. And I never really agreed to do this in the first place, if you'll remember."

Her smile faded. "I know. You have a *life* to lead."

He winced at the quote. "Look, I'm sorry about that, okay?"

She brushed the apology off with a wave of the hand. "Never mind. I am pleased that you're renovating the inn. Ian and I have hated watching it being so shamefully neglected. Just don't allow that woman to paint over our beautiful wood!"

Dean smiled wryly. "So you've said."

Anna looked seriously at him, searching his face with intense eyes, looking for signs that he was the man he appeared to be. "Promise me..."

She heard her own voice fading, felt the odd tugging sensation that signaled her return to the grayness.

"What?" Dean asked, frowning again.

"I have to go now," she said, already sounding farther away, even to herself.

"What did you want me to promise?"

At the moment, one concern overrode all her other worries. "Take care of our home."

He looked surprised. He must have expected her request to have something to do with the other favor she'd asked of him. "I will," he said. There was no mistaking his sincerity. "It's my home, too, now," he reminded her.

She liked the sound of that. It had grieved her that no one had truly loved the inn the way her mother had, the way she and Ian had been raised to love it. Maybe Dean would learn to love it in the same way.

She hadn't understood why Dean was the one who could see her, why she'd never been able to communicate with anyone before him. Maybe the answer lay in their mutual respect for this beautiful place that had been built by her father's own hands.

"Thank you," she whispered.

"You're—"

The grayness suddenly engulfed her.

STANDING IN THE MIDDLE of nowhere, surrounded by nothing, Ian turned to her, obviously relieved that she'd returned. She knew how empty it must seem to him here alone.

"Well?" he asked.

She took his hand and began to tell him everything that had been said. She left out only that odd, intense moment when Dean Gates had looked into her eyes and told her that she was beautiful.

That was a memory to be savored in private.

THERE WAS no indentation on the bed where she'd sat. Dean spread his fingers on the comforter. It was cold.

There was no sign that Anna had ever been here.

Dean sat for a long time with his hand on that empty space beside him, thinking of a young woman with vibrant dark eyes and a smile that made him wish things were different.

5

Life is eternal; and love is immortal; and death is only a horizon; and a horizon is nothing save the limit of our sight.

—Rossiter Worthington Raymond

IT WAS Aunt Mae who'd convinced Dean to attend the library dedication the following Sunday afternoon. She'd heard that almost everyone in town would be there, she said. It would be good for them to mingle with the locals in their new hometown. Though it wasn't exactly Dean's type of affair, he'd agreed because his aunt had seemed to want to attend. She'd worked so hard helping him with the inn. How could he deny her an afternoon of relaxation?

Mae hadn't been exaggerating about the attendance. Whether it was because there was nothing better to do, or because the locals didn't want to risk offending the Peavys, people had turned out in droves. Dean saw quite a few people there he'd already met, and many more he hadn't. The small but nice new library was packed with Peavys, as well as several other prominent citizens.

Margaret Peavy Vandover, the mayor's mother, was as condescendingly gracious as Dean had been led to expect. She'd arrived dramatically late, and Dean had noticed that the cheerful chaos had seemed to subside somewhat upon her entrance. Were the townspeople really as intimidated by the woman as they seemed to be? And, if so, why?

The mayor brought his mother over for introductions. To her credit, she greeted them without visibly reacting to Mae's flowing, bright purple caftan-style dress, worn with the usual profusion of jangling jewelry, and clashing so cheerfully with her copper-tinted hair. Margaret was more conservatively attired in black *moiré* silk and pearls. Though she was probably five to ten years older than Mae, she certainly didn't look it. Dean couldn't help wondering about the efficacy of face-lifts and wrinkle creams.

The painfully thin mayor and his short, plump wife made an amusing couple. She seemed as warm and friendly as he was distant and somber. Dean guessed the mayor owed his office as much to his wife's popularity as to his family's social position.

Roy Peavy, the chief of police, was there, inappropriately attired in uniform. He was a faded, mousy man in his mid-fifties, and Dean suspected he thought the uniform gave him an air of authority he lacked without it. It wasn't hard to guess that his appointment had been the result of blatant nepotism—a small-town tradition.

The most visible Peavy seemed to be Roy's brother, Gaylon, the state representative, named after his great-grandfather. He was surrounded by constituents, many of whom couldn't seem to resist giving him political suggestions to take back to Little Rock. Gaylon had perfected the flashing-smile-hearty-handshake-and-quickly-move-on manner of a career politician, and he worked the room like an expert.

"Interesting group, isn't it?"

Dean turned in response to the drawl, recognizing Mark Winter's voice. He smiled. "Covering the big event?"

"Of course. This is front-page news. The opening of the 'Saint Charles' Library."

Dean chuckled. He'd heard Margaret's dedication speech, and he understood Mark's irony. Dean had almost been nauseated by Margaret's effusive praise of her late father. Talk about obsession!

He took a sip of the too-weak coffee he'd been served in a foam cup. He'd had a choice of the coffee or something green with big chunks of fruit floating in it. The coffee had seemed the safer option.

"I found those notes I promised you," Mark commented. "I'll bring them by tomorrow, okay?"

"Sure. Why don't you stay for dinner?"

"Hey, thanks. If you're sure it's not too much trouble, I'd like that. I get tired of eating take-out."

"No trouble. Aunt Mae loves to entertain. Just remember, the place is a mess, with all the construction going on."

"I'm curious to see how the renovations are coming along."

"We should be ready to open late in July."

"Fast work. No wonder you wanted to get started on your research. When your guests ask about the ghosts—and they will—you'll want to have an answer prepared for them."

"Ghosts?" A portly, pleasant-looking man in a brown suit stepped closer, a curious gleam in his squinty brown eyes. "Have you seen the ghosts?" he asked Dean.

Dean forced a smile. "I'm just curious about the legend," he prevaricated. "I'm Dean Gates, new owner of the Cameron Inn."

The shorter man, who looked to be in his early fifties, pumped Dean's hand enthusiastically.

"R. J. Cooley," he said. "How are you set up for insurance on the place? I'd be happy to look over your policies for ya, and I can probably beat whatever rates you're currently paying. My office is over on Main Street."

Dean smiled, instinctively liking the guy, despite his much-maligned profession. "Let me make a wild guess. You're in insurance."

Mark laughed.

Cooley chuckled. "Yeah. Sorry. Automatic response whenever I meet a new prospect. Got five kids to support and the youngest wants to be an Olympic gymnast. You know how much those lessons cost? Not to mention leotards and tights and competition fees and all that. You . . ."

Mark cleared his throat. "Er, R.J.," he broke in gently. "Why don't you tell Dean about your connection to the local ghosts?"

Apparently unperturbed by the interruption, R.J. promptly changed the subject. "My maternal grandfather, Jeffrey Parker, was engaged to Mary Anna Cameron when she died."

Dean felt something heavy settle in the pit of his stomach. The coffee, most likely. "Engaged?" he repeated.

R.J. nodded. "They announced it the night of the shoot-out, at the twins' twenty-fifth birthday party. Granddad married Gramma Wanda a couple years later and their marriage lasted nearly fifty years, but to tell ya the truth, I don't think he ever really got over his Mary Anna. He didn't talk about her much, but when he did, there was something in his eyes... He called her Anna," R.J added inconsequentially.

The heaviness in Dean's stomach intensified. "Did your grandfather ever tell you about that night?" he asked, trying to sound only casually interested.

"Just once. He and I went fishing up on Lake Ouachita one afternoon, a couple of months before he died. I was about fifteen, and had just been dumped by the head cheerleader. Like to broke my heart. Granddad tried to cheer me up, told me other girls would come along, like Gramma did for him. But he said you never forget that first love."

R.J. lowered his voice. "I got the impression that Granddad and his Anna had had a couple of rowdy nights together... anticipatin' the wedding night, you know. Granddad always seemed fond enough of my grandmother, but I don't think she ever quite measured up in that department. Tell ya the truth, I think Mary Anna was the only really excitin' thing that ever happened in poor old Granddad's long, dull life."

Dean found himself scowling. He forced himself to smile, instead. "It must have been difficult for your grandmother to compete with the memory of a ghost."

"No kidding. Gramma never allowed Mary Anna Cameron's name to be spoken in her presence. They were girlhood chums, I think. Only thing I ever heard her say about it was that she had been greatly deceived about her friend's character."

"So your grandmother believed all the stories about the Cameron twins being bootleggers and murderers."

"Well, sure, most everyone believed it. Stan Tagert caught 'em red-handed, ya know, and he was a respected lawman 'round here 'til he died in a hunting accident about a year after the twins died. Dropped his gun and it discharged, shooting him right in the face. Gaylon and Charles Peavy were hunting with him. They didn't see the accident, but they found the body. Granddad said ol' Gaylon never got over all the tragedies."

"Didn't you once tell me that your grandfather never really believed Mary Anna was involved in anything illegal?" Mark prodded R.J.

"He believed his Mary Anna was an innocent bystander. That she was just in the wrong place at the wrong time. 'Course, he said she'd have done about anything for her brother. She idolized him. Granddad admitted that he was always a little wary of Ian Cameron. Said he had a dangerous look in his eyes."

"So he believed Ian Cameron was a criminal," Dean said thoughtfully.

R.J. shrugged. "Said it wouldn't have surprised him. But not his Anna. He thought *she* was near-perfect."

Dean was getting tired of hearing R.J. refer to Anna as the property of someone else. "*His* Anna." Dean had gotten the impression that Mary Anna Cameron had never belonged to anyone but herself.

"I don't suppose your grandmother is still living," he said, knowing it was probably a futile suggestion.

R.J. shook his head. "Died a few years back, not long after Granddad passed on."

"Is there anyone still living who actually knew the Cameron twins?"

"Not that I know of." R.J. was distracted when someone across the room motioned for him. He made an excuse and left with a final reminder to Dean to bring his insurance policies by for comparison shopping.

Bobbie Vandover, the mayor's cheery wife, approached then, Sharyn Burton in tow. "What are you two boys doing huddled up over here looking so serious when there's a party going on?" she demanded of Dean and Mark. "You both know Sharyn, don't you?"

"Of course," Dean said, nodding politely at the real-estate agent. "How are you, Sharyn?"

Smiling broadly, Sharyn inched close to Dean's side and began to answer his courteous question in more detail than he would have liked. With a grin, Mark left Dean to his fate, making a show of escorting the mayor's wife to the punch bowl for a refill.

Dean tried to put the Cameron twins—one, in particular—out of his mind for the rest of the afternoon, since there was a good chance he'd gotten all the information he was going to get for now.

More than he'd wanted to know, if he were honest with himself.

DEAN TOOK his aunt out for dinner and a movie after the library dedication, still determined to repay her for her hard work. She seemed to enjoy the evening immensely.

By the time Dean kissed her good-night and closed himself into his own bedroom, it was after midnight. He half expected company that evening; he wasn't particularly surprised when Anna arrived.

"Where have you been?" she demanded without preamble as she appeared in the corner of his bedroom.

"That," Dean told her as he finished unbuttoning his shirt, "is none of your business."

He took his shirt off and tossed it over the chair. From what he'd heard earlier, it wouldn't be the first time

Mary Anna Cameron had seen a man without a shirt on.

Anna looked a bit taken aback by his bluntness. "Is something wrong?"

"No." He sat on the edge of the bed to kick off his shoes.

"Would you like me to leave?"

"Yes. No."

He ran a hand through his hair, wishing he knew what he wanted, where Mary Anna Cameron was concerned. He only knew that his feelings toward her were becoming more confused by the day. And that every time he saw her, he was more aware of how beautiful she was. There were parts of him that didn't seem to understand how completely inaccessible she was to him.

She stood with her hands clasped in front of her, watching him closely. "You look tired."

"Yeah. I guess I am." He took a deep breath and looked at her, remembering the favor she'd asked him. "I spent the afternoon at a dedication of the new library. Margaret Peavy Vandover, your stepfather's granddaughter, was there, as well as other descendants of people you knew."

Anna's eyes widened. "Charles's daughter?"

He nodded.

"I remember when she was born. He and his wife were running the inn then. They sold it to that strange couple by the name of Harvey."

"So you've been here at the inn ever since . . . ?"

"Since we died? I told you. Sometimes here. Sometimes at that other place."

"Can you leave the inn? Go into town? Get into a car, maybe?"

"No. Ian tried once. Once we reach the boundary of our property, we find ourselves back at the waiting place."

Dean was too tired to dwell on the oddities of her existence. "Oh."

"Did you find out anything at the dedication? Anything about us, I mean?"

"Very little. I met a man named R. J. Cooley. He's the grandson of Jeffrey Parker." He watched for her reaction as he said the name.

She reacted with a flicker of her eyelashes and a tinge of what might have been a blush on her pale cheeks. "Jeffrey has a grandson?" she asked a bit weakly.

Dean nodded. "R.J. talked about his grandfather and his grandma Wanda."

"Wanda? Wanda Nisbet? Jeffrey *married* her?"

"I don't know her maiden name, but apparently she was a friend of yours."

Anna snorted. "A friend? Hardly. We were rivals from the day we started elementary school. Everything I had, Wanda had to have a better one. Every boyfriend I ever had, she tried to steal. I always thought she was secretly in love with Ian, but he never acknowledged her existence."

"She must have gotten over him. She and Jeff were married for nearly fifty years and had four kids."

Anna's expression turned wistful. "I always knew Jeffrey would make a wonderful father."

"If it makes you feel any better, apparently Jeffrey never really got over you," Dean said grudgingly. "He told his grandson that he had never forgotten you."

Anna's face brightened. "How sweet."

"And he never believed the rumors about you. He thought you were an innocent bystander, in the wrong place at the wrong time."

She beamed. "I'm so glad to hear that. At least *someone* refused to accept those lies about Ian and me."

Dean cleared his throat. "Er—"

She frowned suspiciously. "He did think Ian was innocent, didn't he?"

Dean looked at the ceiling.

Anna stamped her foot. The gesture was no less expressive for being utterly silent. "How could he believe Ian could do those things? You tell Jeffrey that I would have expected more of him."

"Anna, he's dead. Has been for years."

"Oh." She bit her lip. "Of course he is," she said quietly. "Everyone is, aren't they?"

"As far as I've been able to find out. It *has* been seventy-five years. We have to be realistic."

"Didn't you find out anything else today? Wasn't there anyone who believed Ian and I were murdered, and that the real culprit was never unmasked?"

"Mark—the newspaper editor—said there were a few rumors, but for the most part everyone believed the official story, told by the lawman who allegedly caught you and your brother in a secret meeting with a known criminal."

"I heard the story your bleached-blond friend told at your dinner table the other night," Anna said scornfully. "I've heard others give various versions of the same tale. Garbage, all of it. Ian wasn't meeting with Buck Felcher, and he didn't open fire on Stanley Tagert. Ian was walking with me, and he certainly wasn't armed."

"So you're saying Tagert lied. That he was involved in the crime and used you and your brother as scapegoats."

"Exactly. It was Stanley and Buck having the secret meeting. And another man. The one who shot us."

"Buck was also shot and killed," Ian said.

"I heard a third shot just as I lost consciousness," Anna mused. "They must have killed Buck then. Maybe he wasn't cooperating with them. Or maybe they didn't want him as a witness to our murders."

"Who was the third man? The one you say did the shooting?"

She threw up her hands in frustration. "I don't know! If I did, I would have told you by now. Someone murdered us, and Stanley Tagert lied to protect him."

Dean shook his head. "It's hard to believe Tagert could concoct that elaborate a cover-up in such a short time. Surely there were witnesses from the party. People who heard shots, ran to investigate. Questions."

"I don't know," she said curtly. "I wasn't around for a while. By the time Ian and I came back, the investigation was over and everyone seemed to believe the lies. We've been determined ever since to find a way to clear our names. And you're it, Dean. I just know you are."

He rubbed a hand over his face, wondering how he'd ever gotten himself into this mess. "What makes you so sure I'm the one to help you?"

"I've thought about that," she admitted. "Ian keeps asking the same thing. And all I can say is that I have a very strong feeling that you and I were meant to cross paths. There has to be a reason why you can see me, hear me, when others can't. There has to be a purpose."

He sighed. "I'm not so sure. Even if I could find evidence of your innocence—and that's a real long shot, considering how much time has passed—who would believe me? And why would anyone really care, after all this time?"

"Ian and I care," she said quietly. "We care very deeply. Why else do you think we'd still be here?"

He cleared his throat. "Where's Buck? He was apparently murdered at the same time. Didn't he come back with you?"

She shook her head. "We wondered about that for a time. Ian finally decided that since Buck *was* guilty of the crimes he was accused of, there was no reason for him to stay around to clear his name."

That sounded as logical to Dean as anything else that had been presented to him in the past few days. "Tell me exactly what happened that evening, everything you remember," he suggested. "Maybe I'll be able to find something to back up your story."

She started at the beginning. "Ian was outside in the garden, angry about the rumors that had been circulating. I went out to soothe him and to try to entice him back inside . . ."

She gave him the facts concisely, unemotionally, her voice quavering only when she described Ian's death. "And that's all I know," she concluded a few moments later.

"You never saw the face of the third man? Didn't recognize his shape? His voice?"

She shook her head. "Ian and I have discussed this endlessly. Neither of us knows who he was. Both of us have our suspicions."

"Your stepfather?"

Anna went very still. "Why do you say that?"

Dean shrugged. "It's a logical suggestion. Had you lived, the inn would have been yours and your brother's after that night. Gaylon would have lost his comfortable position as manager. With you and Ian out of the way, the inn became his."

"That's what Ian says. He's always believed Gaylon had something to do with our deaths."

"And what about Charles, Gaylon's son?"

Anna spread her hands. "There was no reason for him to hate us. He never seemed all that interested in the inn. He liked to party and carouse with his friends, for the most part. He and Ian never got along, but they were never really enemies, either. I'm afraid Ian didn't get along very well with anyone after our mother died. He was so angry, you see, because he loved her so much and because she died so young."

Anna's face turned sad again. "We weren't even allowed to be with her after our deaths," she murmured.

"I'm sorry," Dean said ineffectually.

"Find our proof, Dean, and maybe we'll be able to see our mother again. Please."

He hated the pressure she was putting on him. "I'll try."

She patted his bare arm. "I know you will. And I want you to know that I appreciate what you're doing for us. You certainly have no obligation. You're a very special man, Dean Gates."

Her touch startled him. It still amazed him that she could touch him, though he had the odd sensation that some thin, cool, invisible barrier lay between them, preventing him from feeling her warmth, her vibrance.

He was intensely aware of the quiet around them. They were alone in his bedroom, just him and this beautiful, intriguing woman, who looked so damned real, so infinitely desirable. It had been a long time since he'd looked at any woman and reacted with a racing pulse and sweating palms.

It was just his luck that the woman who made him feel that way now didn't even *have* a pulse.

She looked at her hand where it lay on his arm. Her expression turned wistful. "I can't feel you," she murmured. "Not really. It's as though I'm touching you through cloth."

"That's pretty much the way it feels to me."

She raised her gaze to his face.

"I wish I could really touch you," she murmured, almost as if to herself. And Dean asked himself if he was only imagining the desire in her voice. A desire very similar to his own.

He couldn't stop looking at her mouth. Wondering how it would feel to kiss a ghost.

"Is, er, your brother here?" he asked, suddenly wondering what it felt like to be punched out by a ghost.

Anna blinked, as though making an effort to concentrate on his question. "Um, no. We've discovered that it's easier, for some reason, for me to contact you when he isn't here. I don't know why. He waits for me to come back and tell you what you've said."

"You seem to be staying longer each time."

"Yes. As I said, it gets easier."

"Can you still see me at times when I can't see you?"

"Sometimes," she admitted. "I have to make an effort for you to see or hear me. Don't ask me to explain how. I can't."

Dean wasn't entirely sure he wanted to ask, anyway. If he started thinking about it too deeply, he'd probably begin to question his sanity again.

Anna lifted her hand from his arm, slowly, and touched her fingertips to his face. It felt odd, but not unpleasant. Not at all unpleasant.

"I have to go now," she said.

"But you'll be back." It wasn't a question.

Dean didn't want to think about how he might feel if she never came back.

She smiled. "Poor Dean. You didn't know what you were getting into when you bought our inn, did you?"

His own smile felt rueful. "No. Not exactly."

"You must be sorry you ever met me."

His smile faded. "No," he said quietly. "I'm not."

Her eyes locked on his face for a moment. Her fingertips brushed his lower lip. "I'm glad," she whispered.

And she was gone.

Dean drew a long breath, then raised a hand to his mouth. He felt strangely as though he'd just been kissed.

It was quiet in his bedroom now. Lonely.

Still wearing his slacks, he lay back on his bed and stared at the ceiling, fantasizing about things that could never be.

Maybe he'd been too long without a woman, he mused. He was finding himself more and more obsessed with a beautiful, dark-eyed ghost.

6

I'd like to get away from earth awhile
And then come back to it and begin over...
Earth's the right place for love.

—Robert Frost

DEAN WAS WORKING outside the next morning, starting the massive task of clearing away some of the deadwood around the garden path. He already had a sizable pile stacked at one corner of the grounds; he would burn it later. Though it was a cold day, he was sweating beneath his flannel shirt and work gloves. He hadn't done hard manual labor in a while, and his muscles were letting him know it.

"Excuse me."

The woman's voice, coming from behind him, made him whirl, his pulse already racing in anticipation. He refused to acknowledge his private disappointment when the woman standing behind him wasn't Anna Cameron, but a rather fragile-looking honey-blonde of about thirty. A little girl of about ten, her own hair so blond it was almost white, stood half-hidden behind the woman, peeking shyly out at Dean.

"Are you Dean Gates?" the woman asked.

"Yes, I am. May I help you?"

"I'm Cara McAlister. This is my daughter, Casey. Mrs. Harper told me we could find you back here."

Dean nodded, waiting for her to get to the point. She looked very nervous, her wide blue eyes darting as though she expected to see danger behind every overgrown bush. Dean hoped heartily that her visit had nothing to do with ghost legends.

She drew a deep breath, as though for courage, and then spoke in a rush of words. "I'm looking for a job," she said. "I've been told you're restoring the inn and hope to open soon. I can help you with the restorations—I've had some experience with decorating. I work very hard, and I'm willing to do anything— painting, cooking, cleaning. All I ask for payment is room and board for myself and my daughter."

Dean was taken completely off guard by the request. Surely the woman could see he was far from ready to hire staff for the inn. He had contractors and subcontractors doing the actual repairwork and he'd already engaged a reputable decorator, his opinion of Ms. Buchanan notwithstanding. As for room and board, he and his aunt occupied the only completed bedrooms. The other two private rooms weren't even furnished.

He opened his mouth to politely tell her he was sorry, he couldn't help her.

But he wasn't given the chance.

"Hire her, Dean." Anna materialized by his side, her attention riveted on the woman and the little girl.

He cleared his throat. "I'm afraid I can't—"

"You can't send her away. Look at her. She looks so tired and so sad. And that precious little girl! They need you."

"Mrs. McAlister," Dean began, trying to ignore the bossy ghost.

The woman lifted her chin in a proud gesture. "I've tried to get a job in town, but there weren't any available," she said. "A waitress at the diner said maybe you would have something."

"She doesn't have anywhere else to go, Dean," Anna piped in. "I have a feeling about her. She needs help. Ian could tell you—if you could hear him—my feelings are always right."

"I don't even have a room ready," Dean muttered, frustrated that he couldn't talk to Anna without looking like a head case. "I just moved into the inn, myself, a couple of weeks ago. We're a long way from being ready for guests *or* staff."

"Casey and I don't need special accommodations. We'll share a room, sleep on cots, sleeping bags, whatever. I'd like to help you get the inn ready to open."

"Don't send her away, Dean," Anna urged.

Dean was beginning to feel trapped. This was crazy. He didn't need a cook or a maid or a live-in decorator. And an inn in the middle of renovations was no place for a little girl. Despite Anna's prodding, he was all set to turn the woman away.

And then he looked into her eyes.

Cara McAlister wasn't exactly begging—Dean had the impression she wasn't the type—but she was as close as a proud woman could come to doing so. He could see the desperation, and the despair. "I'll work very hard," she repeated.

He sighed. "When do you want to start?"

Her eyes lit up. "Our things are all in the car. We can move in immediately."

"Poor dears. They don't even have a home," Anna murmured.

Dean flicked her a glance, then turned back to the other woman. His new employee.

"We'll have to see about getting some furniture in one of the extra bedrooms. There are some old beds and chests stored in one of the rooms upstairs. I'll haul a couple down for you until we can come up with something better. Aunt Mae's been doing all the cooking and has started cleaning the parts of the inn that are ready. You can work with her. We'll discuss salary later."

Cara gave him a shy, grateful smile. "Thank you. You won't regret it."

He sincerely hoped she was right. He nodded toward the child. "Make sure she stays away from the construction crews. It would be dangerous for her to be around them when they're working."

"She'll stay out of their way," Cara promised.

The little girl nodded in agreement. Dean wondered if she was always so quiet and subdued. He couldn't help questioning what this odd couple was running from. That they were running from something was obvious. The most logical explanation was an abusive husband and father. Dean stifled a sigh, asking himself how much more complicated his life was going to get since he'd "simplified" it by buying the inn.

He glanced at his watch. It was just after noon. He'd bet Cara and Casey hadn't eaten lunch, maybe not even breakfast. He would also bet Aunt Mae was already in the kitchen, preparing food for them.

"Why don't the two of you go inside to Aunt Mae for something to eat," he suggested. "I'll put away my tools and be right in."

Cara nodded, took her daughter's hand and turned away. She paused at the end of the path and looked back over her shoulder. "Thank you, Mr. Gates."

He nodded, uncomfortable with the hint of tears in her voice. "Yeah," he said gruffly. "Go have something to eat."

"You really are a sweet man," Anna said approvingly when they were alone. "I had a feeling about you from the first."

"Let's just hope your 'feelings' don't get me in a truckload of trouble," he said bluntly. "Damn it, Anna, I don't need her here. What am I supposed to do with her?"

"The inn needs maids," she said with an innocent expression. "We always had at least three on staff."

"The inn isn't even open. It won't be for several months."

"Then she can cook and clean for you and your aunt while you prepare to open. I've worried about your aunt doing all that heavy cleaning she's been taking on. Did you know she was up on a ladder yesterday, dusting fixtures?"

Dean scowled. "No. I didn't know that." He would definitely have to talk to Aunt Mae. She had no business being on a ladder with her bad knees. Of course, he'd have to figure out a way to tell her how he knew about her behavior without having actually seen her.

It occurred to him that he was taking Anna's presence much more for granted now. It no longer even startled him when she made her appearances. And he spent entirely too much time anticipating her doing so.

"I like your aunt. She seems very kind."

He nodded. "She is. She raised my sister and me after our parents died in a car crash when we were kids."

Anna's face lit up. "You have a sister? Is she a twin?"

He shook his head. "She's eight years younger. She was here with me once, when I was looking over the inn."

"I must have missed her. Are you close to her?"

"Yes, we're quite close."

Anna smiled. "That's nice. Ian and I have always been best friends. I can't imagine being separated from him."

"About this woman you coerced me into hiring—"

Anna giggled. "I didn't coerce you. How could I?"

He gave her an expressive look. "You have your ways. But what if you're wrong about her? I know nothing about her. She could be a thief, a con artist, a drunk, a lazy sponger."

Anna was shaking her head. "She's none of those things. She's only a nice woman who's fallen onto hard times."

"Do your supernatural powers include mind reading?" Dean asked.

She looked at him reprovingly. "Of course not. I just—"

"—have a feeling," he finished with her.

She smiled again. "Exactly."

He shook his head.

Anna laughed. The musical sound made his chest tighten. God, she was beautiful when she smiled. Or when she frowned. Or when she looked angry. Or sad.

Anna searched his face, and her smile faded. He didn't know what she saw in his expression, but she took a gliding step closer. "Dean?"

"Dean?" Mae called his name as she made her way carefully down the partially cleared walkway. "Lunch is ready. What are you doing out here?" she asked, looking curiously at what was now empty space beside him. "What are you looking at so intently?"

Dean drew his gaze reluctantly away from the spot where Anna had stood. "Sorry, Aunt Mae. I was just thinking about how much more has to be done out here."

"You've made quite a lot of headway since I was out last," his aunt said approvingly. And then she lost interest in the landscaping and faced him again, wearing a rather smug smile.

"I knew you would hire her," she said without bothering to clarify who she meant. "As soon as I saw her and that dear little girl, and heard her explain that she needed a job and a home, I knew you wouldn't be able to turn her away."

"I must have lost my mind," Dean muttered. "This is the worst possible time for me to hire a maid. And as for the kid, heaven only knows what we'll do with her."

"We'll take care of her—of both of them. They need us, Dean. I knew that immediately. The little girl reminds me of Bailey, when you and she first came to live with me. She looks a little sad, and a little lost. So very vulnerable."

In resignation, Dean realized that his softhearted aunt had just adopted two more strays into their family.

And he'd thought being a small-town innkeeper would be a nice, easy, "normal" life!

MARK WINTER was expected for dinner that evening. When Cara heard that Mae and Dean were anticipating a guest, she immediately volunteered to prepare and serve the meal.

"There's no need for you to start working so soon," Mae protested. "You just got your car unloaded."

Dean had spent a couple of hours after lunch hauling furniture, setting up twin beds and a large chest of drawers in one of the empty, but freshly painted downstairs bedrooms, helping Cara bring her few possessions in from the aging, battered vehicle in which she'd arrived. Cara had worked right by his side, reserved, but eager to do her share, while little Casey had hovered close by, watching intently.

He knew Cara had to be tired; frankly, she didn't look as though she'd had a good night's sleep in quite a while. "Aunt Mae's right, Cara," he told her. "There's no need for you to start today. Why don't you join us for dinner as our guest? You and Casey both, of course," he added with a smile for the child, who smiled shyly in return.

Cara shook her head, her face taking on a stubborn set that Dean predicted would soon be very familiar to him. "I earn my way," she said quietly. "And I like to cook. You and your aunt enjoy your evening with your friend. Casey and I will eat in the kitchen."

Nothing either Dean or Mae could say would change her mind. They finally conceded when it looked as though Cara was becoming upset with them.

Mark arrived promptly, carrying a thick manila envelope, which he handed to Dean. "I made you a copy of everything I had about the Cameron twins," he explained. "It's not much, I'm afraid, but it's a start."

"Thanks, Mark. I'll go through it later."

"Sure." Having already greeted Mae, Mark turned back to her with a smile. "It's very nice of you to go to the trouble of having me for dinner, Mrs. Harper. It's been a coon's age since I had a home-cooked meal. I've been looking forward to it all day."

Her multiple bracelets tingling merrily, Mae patted him on the arm in a naturally maternal gesture. "We're delighted to have you. As for the meal, it's been no trouble for me at all. Dean's new housekeeper prepared it."

Mark lifted an eyebrow. "You've hired a housekeeper already?" he asked, looking pointedly around at the unfinished lobby.

Dean shrugged. "She showed up on the doorstep, asking for a job. My, er, conscience insisted that I hire her."

Across the room, Mary Anna Cameron laughed softly. Glancing at her warningly, Dean wondered how long she'd been there.

If she did anything to make him look foolish this evening, he would—he would—well, there wasn't a hell of a lot he could do about it. But he'd damned well let her know it if she made him mad.

"Is the new housekeeper someone from town?" Mark asked.

Dean shook his head. "She said she's new in these parts. She looked for a job in Destiny, but couldn't find anything. Someone at the diner sent her here."

"There aren't many jobs in Destiny these days," Mark commiserated. "Unless you're related to the Peavys, of course."

Dean and his aunt led their guest to the dining room, explaining that they would eat first and then move to the sitting room for an after-dinner visit. Mark heartily concurred with the plan.

Cara was just putting the finishing touches to the table setting when they walked into the small, private dining room. Dean noted immediately that the table looked beautiful; Aunt Mae's best silver, china, linen napkins and lace tablecloth, burning tapers, fresh flowers in a heavy crystal bowl. Since he and his aunt had been dining very casually—paper-plate casually—the past few weeks, it was a pleasant change.

Mark looked suitably impressed. "Hey, you've got this room looking really nice," he said. "If this is a sample of what you'll be doing in the rest of the inn, you'll . . ."

His voice suddenly faded away.

Dean realized that in response to Mark's voice, Cara had straightened and turned toward him. Mark seemed to have forgotten what he was saying.

Dean smothered a smile. It was apparent that Mark had been startled by Cara's delicate blond beauty. No surprise. Dean might have been struck speechless, himself, had he not become recently obsessed with a dark-haired, dark-eyed vision.

"Isn't that sweet?" the vision in question murmured from close to Dean's side. "He looks as though someone just hit him over the head with a club."

Ignoring Anna, Dean stepped forward to make the introductions. "Cara McAlister, this is Mark Winter, the owner and editor of the local newspaper."

Cara had smiled politely when the others had entered the room. Her smile suddenly faded, leaving an expression that Dean thought was a mixture of consternation and distaste. "You're a journalist?" she asked.

Mark nodded with a wry smile. "'Fraid so. It's a dirty job, but someone's gotta do it."

She didn't return the smile. "Dinner is ready if you'd like to be seated now," she said to the room at large. And then she turned and disappeared into the kitchen.

"Oh, my," Anna murmured. "I don't think she cares for journalists."

"No kidding," Dean muttered, having already reached that inevitable conclusion.

Mark closed his mouth and looked at Dean. "Er, was it something I said?"

Dean shrugged and motioned toward the table. "Have a seat," he said without answering Mark's rueful question.

Dean held a chair for his aunt, then took his own place.

"Well?" Anna demanded in teasingly feigned outrage. "Aren't you going to hold a seat for *me*?"

And wouldn't my guest love to see that? Dean thought wryly. He could imagine the next day's headlines: Town's Newest Resident Dines With Imaginary Friend.

Or worse: Cameron Ghosts Make Reappearance. Wouldn't *that* bring out the lunatics and tabloid hounds?

"Never mind," Anna said with a laugh. "I can see you'd rather pretend I'm not here at all."

That wasn't true, actually. Dean would very much like to acknowledge her presence. He just wished he could do so under normal circumstances.

"Will Ms. McAlister be joining us for dinner?" Mark asked, his eyes straying toward the kitchen door.

"We asked her to, of course, but she and her daughter prefer to eat in the kitchen this evening," Mae explained. "I suppose they're tired after moving in today and then preparing our meal."

"Her daughter?" Mark repeated.

Mae nodded. "She's a single mother. Her little girl, Casey, is ten years old. Pretty, like her mother."

Mark looked thoughtful.

"Do you think he likes children?" Anna asked Dean.

He shrugged faintly. Anna seemed to have a bit of matchmaking in mind. Why couldn't she be content with haunting *him?* If she thought she was going to sweet-talk him into helping her get Mark and Cara together, she had another—

Cara entered the room then, carrying a heavy tray. Mark almost broke his neck jumping out of his chair to help her. She thanked him coolly, never meeting his eyes.

Dean risked giving Anna a wry look. Couldn't she see that Cara wasn't interested in Mark?

She gave him a smile in return that he couldn't begin to interpret.

Conversation flowed easily enough during dinner, though Mark seemed rather distracted, his gaze often straying to the closed door that led into the kitchen.

Of course, Mark wasn't the only one having trouble keeping his mind off a woman. Dean had his hands full carrying on a coherent conversation with his aunt and Mark without visibly reacting to Anna's frequent observations. She drifted around the room throughout the meal, first in one corner, then another, making Dean dizzy with her movements. He wished he could order her to stay in one place.

Mark told them about the newest computer equipment he hoped to buy for the newspaper soon, his conversation becoming quite technical after a while.

"Do you actually understand what he's talking about?" Anna inquired incredulously, staring at Mark as though he were speaking Greek. Dean supposed "compuspeak" must sound like a foreign language to a young woman who'd lived at the turn of the century. Even Aunt Mae seemed hard-pressed to follow the conversation, and she had some familiarity with modern technology, though of course, not nearly as much as Mark and Dean had.

He nodded subtly, then tried to pay attention as Mark changed the subject to world events. An avid TV-news junkie, Mae was clearly much more at ease with this conversation, and soon she and Mark were enthusiastically debating national politics, rapidly finding points on which they agreed and cheerfully disagreed. Dean added a word or two, but spent most of the time watching Anna's changing expressions as she tried to follow the conversation.

"Goodness," she said with a shake of her dark head. "Things surely have changed."

"You don't know the half of it," Dean risked murmuring into his water glass.

Her expression became wistful. "I'd like to see more of this new world."

Dean couldn't reply—even if he had known what to say.

They moved into the private sitting room after dinner. Though they'd asked Cara to join them, she had politely refused, conspicuously avoiding Mark's eyes. She explained that she was tired, and as soon as she finished clearing away the dishes, she and Casey were turning in. Mae insisted on going into the kitchen to help with the cleaning, though Cara protested.

Dean smiled. Cara would soon learn how useless it was to argue with his aunt when she wore that particular look on her sweetly lined face.

"So tell me about Cara," Mark said as soon as he and Dean were alone in the sitting room, steaming mugs of coffee in hand. "You say she just appeared out of nowhere and asked for a job?"

Dean nodded. "That's right. No references, no history. Just a little girl at her side and a needy look in her eyes."

"She's running from something," Mark murmured.

"An abusive husband, unless I miss my guess," Dean agreed.

Mark winced. "Yeah, most likely."

"I figured it isn't any of my business, unless some jerk shows up and starts making trouble, of course."

Mark's face darkened. "If that happens, give me a call. I'll help you take care of him."

Dean murmured something noncommittal and took a sip of his coffee.

"He's very taken with her," Anna commented, standing close to Mark and studying his face. "Do you think she *is* married?"

Dean had wondered if Anna was going to join them in the sitting room. He lifted one shoulder in a slight shrug, gave her a look to remind her that he wasn't at liberty to talk freely to her, then turned back to Mark.

"I appreciate your bringing those notes by this evening," he said, knowing Anna would be interested. "Are you sure you never found anything to indicate that events here happened any differently than everyone says?"

As he'd expected, Anna moved closer, listening intently.

Mark shook his head. "What I found was very sketchy," he admitted. "I interviewed a few locals, dug up some old newspapers, tried to get my hands on some official documents."

"And . . . ?"

"And—not much," Mark said. "The locals all gave me various versions of the same story, with some individual exaggerations. The newspaper articles were oddly uninformative, considering the scope of the story. And no official documents appear to have survived."

Dean frowned. "Surely there are some old police reports. Something."

"Not according to what I was told. Most of the records were apparently lost in a tornado back in the fifties."

"And the newspaper articles?"

"Simply stated that Ian and Mary Anna Cameron, local residents, were killed in a shoot-out with Deputy Stanley Tagert when he tried to arrest them for bootlegging and other suspected crimes. Their stepfather and Mary Anna's fiancé both declared themselves too grief-stricken to be interviewed, their friends clammed up, a couple of attention-grabbing neighbors claimed they'd known all along that Ian Cameron was a criminal."

"Lies!" Anna exclaimed. "All lies."

"There has to be something more," Dean muttered. "Someone had to know what really happened."

"Stanley Tagert knew," Anna insisted. "As well as whoever pulled the trigger on Ian and Buck and me."

"Stanley Tagert died on a hunting trip about a year after the shootings. That left only the third man alive," Dean told her, forgetting just for that one moment that he shouldn't be speaking to her. "*He's* the one we have to identify, though I don't know how we're going to do it."

"Third man?" Mark looked in bewilderment from Dean to the apparently empty corner toward which Dean seemed to be staring. "What third man?"

Dean frowned, embarrassed with his gaffe. "I, er, have reason to believe that Tagert may have been in on the crime and that Ian and Mary Anna died because they saw something they shouldn't have."

Mark looked skeptical. "Why do you think that? How could you possibly know anything about this, especially since you've only lived in these parts a short time?"

Dean groped for something to say, looking to Anna for suggestions. For once, she was quiet, shrugging apologetically.

"You *have* found something, haven't you? A diary? A journal? What is it, damn it?"

"I—" Dean started to deny it, then changed his mind. "I *have* come across something," he admitted. "But I'm not at liberty to tell you about it now. Not until I have more evidence."

"Evidence of what?"

"Evidence that the Peavy family fortune is founded on murder. Probably bootlegging."

"Oh, man," Mark groaned. "You are going to stir up a hornet's nest if you start making that claim around here. You don't know how prickly Margaret Peavy Vandover is when it comes to her family honor. Not to mention the senator, the mayor and the chief of police. These people have power around here, Dean. You have no idea how difficult they can make things for you if they set their minds to it—especially Margaret."

"I'm aware of that. Why do you think I'm looking for more proof before I say anything?"

"Even if you find the proof," Mark said, "why would you bother to bring it out now? Isn't it possible that you'd be harming innocent descendants of wrong-doers, rather than exacting justice? I know this is a strange question coming from a so-called journalist, but why would you want to break a story like this when there's no one alive who really cares?"

Anna flinched.

Dean resisted an impulse to reach out to her. "Are you saying that if you had the evidence to clear the Cameron twins' names, you wouldn't release it because it might offend the Peavy family?" he asked Mark, instead.

Mark hesitated, then shrugged. "I guess I've gotten soft. I know what it's like to destroy a family's reputation, Dean. Especially when there's a politician in the family. I destroyed a few during my stint as an investigative reporter for a statewide newspaper. There was one man in particular—the state's attorney general. I found out about the mistress he was keeping, despite his image as a devoted husband and family man. He was supporting her, of course, with taxpayers' money. I broke the story. His family disintegrated, and his Bible-belt political career crashed and burned."

Mark rubbed a hand over his face in a weary gesture. "The hell of it was, he was basically a decent man. Dedicated public servant. Performed his job competently, efficiently, honestly, except for that one failing. I'd always admired him. Still do. And I still wonder if it was really anyone's business that he fell in love with the wrong woman at the wrong time."

"For seventy-five years," Dean said gently, "Ian and Mary Anna Cameron have been branded as criminals. Murderers. They've become the local ghost story to be bandied about around campfires. If there's even a chance that they were innocent, that someone murdered them and got away with it, don't you think someone should try to clear their names?"

"That someone being you?"

Dean cleared his throat, aware of Anna's gaze on his face. "Well, yeah, I guess so."

"So you're—what? Trying to lay troubled souls to rest?"

Dean tried to return Mark's wry smile. "Something like that, I suppose."

"You're sure you haven't seen the ghosts, yourself?"

Dean hoped his smile didn't look as sickly as it felt. "Haven't heard nary a rattling chain," he drawled in an affected Southern accent that made Mark grimace.

Mark's smile faded then and he sighed. "Tell you what, Dean. You find evidence of any sort that the Cameron twins were falsely accused, and I'll run the story. It's certainly a story of local interest, whether the Peavy family was involved or not. But I'm going to need more than your hunches—or the ghostly whisperings of a tormented spirit."

Anna glared at Mark. "That wasn't funny."

"I'll try to find you something more concrete," Dean agreed. "And, Mark, I'm not taking this lightly. I have no interest in stirring up trouble just for the fun of it, or hurting innocent people. I just want to know the truth about the history of my new home."

"Fair enough, I suppose."

Mae joined them then, and the men let the subject drop. The next time Dean looked toward Anna's corner, she was gone.

He wondered whether she approved of what he'd done thus far to help her.

7

All that we see or seem
Is but a dream within a dream.

—Edgar Allan Poe

ANNA DIDN'T REAPPEAR during the next week. Dean wondered if she'd stayed too long Monday evening. Maybe she was off in that gray waiting area with her brother, gaining strength to return.

Or maybe he would never see her again. That possibility was a constant, nagging worry at the back of his mind.

It wasn't so bad during the daytime, when he could stay busy with the renovations and his attempts at researching the inn's history. He had put together a chronology of the inn's ownership since the twins' deaths. Their stepfather, Gaylon, had managed it until his death in 1939, at which time his son, Charles, had taken over. Eleven years later, Charles sold the inn to a man named Jonas Harvey, who'd kept it four years before running into financial difficulties.

In 1954, the inn was purchased by a bohemian art group, who used it for a creative retreat funded by wealthy patrons. The group disbanded five years later and the inn was closed. It reopened in 1961, purchased by a nostalgic former member of the art group, and had limped along until 1974 when it had closed again.

Taking advantage of the bicentennial historical fervor, the inn reopened in 1976, owned and managed by a devoted member of the Daughters of the American Revolution. It thrived for a few years, particularly during the early-winter horse-racing season at nearby Hot Springs, but then had been forced to close due to tax problems.

Two more owners had briefly tried and failed to recapture the inn's former financial success. It had been closed for almost six years when some odd twist of fate had brought it to Dean's attention.

He read every archival article he could get his hands on, but they were few and unsatisfactory. Even the state newspapers had had little to say about the incident of February 14, 1921; so much had been going on in the world at that time that little attention was given to the deaths of a suspected small-town bootlegger, his sister and his alleged partner.

He talked to the locals. In the diner, the market, the barbershop, the gas station—anyone who was willing to discuss the old scandal became a potential source of information. Dean found more than a few townspeople willing to speculate about Gaylon Peavy's role in the tragedy, but that was all he got from them. Speculation. What ifs. Maybes. Nothing that even began to prove Ian Cameron's innocence.

If there ever had been a serious investigation into any scenario other than the one Tagert had given after the shootings, Dean found no evidence of it. Some of the old-timers recalled that Tagert hadn't been particularly popular, but none of them had ever heard talk that he'd been crooked.

Despite his frustration with his lack of progress into the investigation, Dean was fascinated by the developing picture of the inn's history, and the people whose lives it had touched. As full as they were, the days passed quickly.

The nights, however, were long and restless. He slept in snatches, waking often to look blearily around his room, making sure he was alone. Always vaguely disappointed to find that he was.

"You really are an idiot, Gates," he muttered late Wednesday afternoon, when he realized he was all but drooping with exhaustion from the amount he'd done on so little sleep.

"Talking to yourself again, Dean?" his aunt inquired as she approached in the garden where he was ripping down a rotten latticework trellis. He was taking advantage of a relatively balmy late-January afternoon to get some outside work done.

Dean chuckled. "Yeah. This time, I was."

"You'd better watch that. People could start to worry about you. In fact, maybe they already have." Her eyes searched his face as she spoke, and Dean knew she saw the lines and shadows of weariness.

"Just tired, Aunt Mae. We knew it would be a big job, getting the inn ready to open."

"I can't help feeling that there's something more."

He avoided her eyes. "I'm fine. Really. How are things going inside?"

Pulling her brightly embroidered jacket more tightly around her against the light, chilly breeze, Mae watched as Dean, clad in a sweatshirt, jeans and work gloves, reached for another section of trellis. "Well enough. It's certainly noisy in there now, with the carpenters at work upstairs. Poor Casey. Every loud noise makes her jump. She's a timid little dear, isn't she?"

Dean knew that his aunt had all but adopted Casey, the same way she had adopted him and his sister. In return, Casey adored the woman she already called Aunt Mae.

Only with Mae had Dean seen the child relax and giggle the way a little girl her age should. With him, she was polite, but extremely shy. With her mother, she seemed anxious to please, as though she were the caretaker and her mother the one needing nurturing.

"Cara still working her fingers off in there?" Dean asked, already knowing the answer.

Mae sighed. "I'm afraid so. I simply can't get her to slow down. She's even tackled some of the heavy jobs we plan to hire people to do. She's determined to earn her way."

Dean shook his head. "She's certainly doing that. I don't suppose she's told you any more about herself?"

"No, she hasn't. I haven't pried, of course, but I've made it clear that she's among friends now, and if she ever needs to talk, either of us would provide a sympathetic ear."

"Mark's called me twice asking how she's doing," Dean commented.

"He did seem to be rather taken with her, didn't he? But I'm afraid I got the distinct impression she isn't interested in dating anyone. For all we know, she isn't even free to do so."

"I just hope we don't have any other strays showing up on our doorstep," Dean said ruefully. "Between us and the McAlisters, the inn's already getting full, and we haven't even opened yet."

"Not to mention the Cameron twins," Mae agreed cheerfully.

Dean dropped a board solidly on his foot.

He jumped, cursed, then looked questioningly at his aunt. "The, er, Cameron twins?" he asked, wondering if Anna had been visiting with someone else in the inn since he'd last seen her.

Mae laughed. "Of course. Our very own ghosts. They seem to come up in conversation with everyone I talk to in town. They're very popular around here, you know. I suppose every little town likes having its own ghost stories with which to spook the schoolchildren."

Dean could just imagine Anna's reaction to *that!* He found himself surreptitiously looking around, half expecting her to appear and protest.

There was no sign of her.

He sighed and went back to work.

THE CLOCK on the nightstand read 2:51 when he woke. His dreams had been . . . disturbing, leaving him itchy and aching and covered with a light film of sweat. He didn't allow himself to dwell on the details. He knew exactly what he'd been doing in the dream, and with whom.

The inn was utterly silent, sleeping. Dean looked automatically toward the corner where Anna had appeared once before. This time, the chair was only a chair. No haunting eyes met his, there was no beaming smile to tighten his chest and make him think longingly of stolen kisses and intimate murmurings.

He was alone. And aware of his loneliness as he hadn't been in a very long time.

He rolled over in the bed, one arm bent under his head, and stared at the wall.

He was used to sleeping alone. His marriage had been over some time before it formally ended, and he and Gloria had moved into separate bedrooms. Since his divorce, he simply hadn't had the energy to pursue another relationship, finding it easier to devote his efforts to starting a new life.

Whatever he'd felt for Gloria in the beginning had been strong, hot, exciting, but it hadn't lasted. He no longer believed in the lifelong romantic love celebrated in songs and fiction.

Of course, until a few weeks ago, he hadn't believed in ghosts, either.

Exhaling gustily, he snapped on the bedside lamp. He wouldn't fall back to sleep anytime soon; he might as well read until he was feeling sleepy again. He reached for the mystery novel on the nightstand, but found himself picking up the small, framed photograph that had been lying beside it.

Mary Anna Cameron's face smiled back at him from behind the slightly yellowed glass of the old frame. His chest grew tight.

He'd "borrowed" the photograph from his aunt with the excuse that he wanted to use it as a reference in his remodeling of the inn. He'd known then that he was lying. He hadn't looked at the building in the picture since he'd brought the photo into his room. His only interest had been in the woman.

Anna.

"Damn it," he muttered, glaring at her as though she could answer from the snapshot. "Where *are* you?"

The only reply was the silence of the night.

TWO MORE DAYS passed without a visit from Anna, though not without other visitors. Mark Winter dropped by, supposedly to give Dean a few more sketchy notes on the inn's background, but it was obvious his only reason for being there was to see Cara

McAlister again. Cara treated him exactly as she had on the previous occasion. Polite, but distant. *Very* distant.

Mark didn't linger long, nor did Dean encourage him to. He only hoped his friendship with the publisher wouldn't be affected by Mark's inconvenient infatuation with the housekeeper.

The next day, the mayor and his wife stopped in using as their excuse the desire to look over the renovations and keep abreast of the developments of the town's newest business. Aunt Mae and the mayor's bubbly wife huddled over cups of tea for a cozy gossip while Dean and the mayor braved the blustery weather for a walk around the grounds and more stilted conversation.

"It's looking really good," Mayor Vandover conceded. "The work is proceeding faster than I would have thought possible."

"We've been lucky," Dean agreed. "The weather and suppliers all seem to be cooperating."

"It's been a mild winter so far. They say that means we're in for one hell of a hot summer. Brace yourself, Gates. Summers around here can be rough for someone from up north."

"I spent most of the summers of my childhood at my grandparents' home just outside of Atlanta," Dean explained with a stiff smile. "I know how humid it gets down here."

Vandover nodded. "Back when I was a toddler, and my grandfather still ran this inn, everyone thought this garden was the most beautiful place in the world in the summertime."

He motioned around toward the half cleared tangle of weeds and dead greenery. "The roses were spectacular. My great-grandfather's second wife, Amelia, planted them. Over the years, as the inn changed hands several times, the gardens were allowed to fall into decay. No one seemed to care about them."

"I plan to hire a landscaper this spring to rework the gardens. I don't know if I can compete with Amelia's roses, but I can certainly make it look better than this."

Vandover looked toward the old shack at the edge of the woods. "Better clear that rubble away before guests arrive," he advised a bit pompously. "If someone strays in there and gets hurt, you'll have a hell of a lawsuit on your hands."

"I intend to," Dean said with forced patience. "All of the outbuildings are going to come down. Especially that one."

Vandover lifted an eyebrow. "Guess you've heard that's the site of the infamous shoot-out."

"I've heard."

"Some folks think it ought to be preserved. A historical landmark, you know. I don't agree. Sooner our town forgets about that ugly incident, the better, as far as I'm concerned. It's been an embarrassment to my family for seventy-five years."

"Oh?" Dean asked blandly. "And why is that?"

"Well, the twins were my great-grandfather's stepkids. No kin to the rest of us, of course, but still, nobody likes admitting there were bootleggers and murderers even casually connected to their family."

"A lot of today's great fortunes were founded on bootlegging," Dean said, keeping his expression neutral. "And probably murder, as well, if the truth were known."

Vandover shot a suspicious look at him and muttered something incomprehensible.

"Whatever happened to all the money Ian Cameron supposedly made with his illicit activities?" Dean asked as though the thought had just occurred to him. "Did anyone ever find a stash buried in the basement or under a rock somewhere?"

Vandover frowned. "Not as far as I know. I never really gave it a thought. Why? You think you might come upon it when you dig up the rose garden?"

Dean forced a smile. "One never knows."

The mayor shook his head. "I'd forget about it, if I were you. Best for you to rename the place and start afresh. Forget you ever heard about the Cameron twins."

That, of course, was a lot easier said than done, Dean reflected as he led the mayor back inside the inn. He didn't think anyone who'd encountered the enchanting Mary Anna Cameron could ever forget her.

SOMETIME IN THE MIDDLE of that long, restless night, he half convinced himself he'd dreamed her all along. If she really had existed, why hadn't he seen her again? If she'd learned to contact him at will, why hadn't she checked back with him to inquire about his progress in the investigation of her death?

Or *was* she still hanging about, watching him in silence, staying out of his view for reasons of her own?

It was enough to make a man question his sanity.

Whether he'd dreamed her before or not, she seemed destined to invade his dreams now. Several times he woke again in a light sweat, his pulse racing, his mind filled with erotic images of himself and a woman with cool skin and dark eyes. A woman he found himself wanting with an intensity he'd never known.

The one woman he shouldn't want.
Where was she?

SHARYN BURTON popped in the next afternoon, this time bearing a loaf of fresh-baked banana nut bread. It was obvious that she had already heard about the new housekeeper.

"So," she asked Dean a bit too casually over coffee in the sitting room, "is she someone you've known a while?"

Impatient to get back to the work he'd been doing outside, Dean shook his head. "No," he said without elaborating.

His aunt had been with them until a few moments before, when she'd been called to the telephone. Dean was acutely aware of being alone with Sharyn; mostly because *she* seemed so very much aware of it. Dean wondered how soon he could politely get away.

"Dean," Sharyn said after taking a deep breath, "I was wondering if you would like to have dinner with me one night this week."

He swallowed. He certainly wasn't surprised by the move; he'd just hoped he would be able to avoid it.

"Er, thanks, Sharyn, but I'm afraid I can't right now. It isn't a good time for me."

She made no effort to hide her disappointment. "I hope I haven't embarrassed you."

"Not at all," he assured her. "It's just—"

"Still stinging from the divorce?" she suggested.

He decided to give her that. "Yeah, that's it," he said too eagerly. "It hasn't been very long."

She sighed. "I felt the same way after my marriage ended. They say the best thing to do is get right into the dating scene, but some people seem to need more time to heal."

"Yeah. I'm still . . . healing."

He felt like a jerk for lying to her, but he simply couldn't think of another way to let her know that he wasn't interested.

Sharyn smiled graciously. "If you change your mind . . ."

He nodded. "Thanks."

She didn't stay long after that.

Dean gave a sigh of relief. Truth was, he didn't want to be with *any* woman right now. But even as that thought crossed his mind, he knew he was lying to himself. The real problem was, the only woman he could want was the one woman he would never—*could* never—have.

Dean wasn't in any hurry to turn in that evening. He wasn't ready to face another night of lying awake, waiting for a visit that didn't come.

Everyone else had already gone to bed, leaving him in the sitting room, watching old sitcom reruns on cable. Growing bored with the idealistic, black-and-white worlds depicted there, he turned the TV off and wandered into the kitchen, thinking maybe a glass of milk would help him sleep.

Someone was sitting in the kitchen, silent and dressed all in white.

For a moment, his pulse jerked. "An—"

He stopped when he saw the honey-blond hair.

"Cara," he said after a moment, trying to make his voice sound normal, trying to hide his disappointment. "What are you doing up at his hour?"

She whirled, one hand on her heart, the other clasping the front of her thick white robe. "Oh! You startled me."

"I'm sorry. I didn't know anyone was in here. Are you all right?"

"Yes, I'm fine. I couldn't sleep and I thought I'd have a glass of milk."

He smiled. "Great minds," he murmured without bothering to finish the saying. "That's what I was going to do."

She gave him a shy smile. "I'll pour two glasses."

"Thanks." He opened the pantry door. "How about a cookie to go with it? Milk seems kinda lonely without a cookie."

She chuckled. "Maybe just one."

He grabbed a handful of cream-filled chocolate cookies. She was too thin. A few extra calories wouldn't hurt her.

Setting three cookies in front of her, he took a chair on the opposite side of the small kitchen table. Then he tried to think of something to say. It was the first time he and Cara had actually been alone.

"So, how's Casey settling in?" he asked lamely, figuring talking about her daughter would make her feel comfortable.

Cara smiled. "Just fine. She's fallen hard for your aunt, you know."

"Everyone does. Aunt Mae's one of a kind."

"She's been helping Casey with her lessons in the afternoons. I wasn't really surprised to learn that she's a retired schoolteacher."

Dean knew his aunt had been concerned when she'd learned that Cara had been home-schooling Casey with correspondence materials, though she'd told him that Casey seemed to be on an average level for her age. It worried Mae that Casey was such an isolated child, with no companionship of children her own age. Dean tended to agree with his aunt.

"You, uh, haven't thought about putting Casey into Destiny Elementary?" Dean asked, wondering if she would find the question intrusive. "I've been told it's a good school."

"I have thought about it," Cara admitted. "I'm worried about her not having any playmates. It's just that we've moved around so much during the past year, it seemed easier to try to teach her myself."

"You have a home and a job here for as long as you need one," Dean told her, touched by the wistfulness in Cara's voice. "Assuming, of course, that we don't all end up homeless if the inn goes bust," he added ruefully.

She smiled, her blue eyes luminous. "I don't think that will happen," she murmured. "Something tells me you make a success of whatever you take on."

"I try."

She finished her milk and two of the cookies, pushing the third toward him. "I'd better go to bed," she said. "Maybe I'll visit the school tomorrow."

"I'm sure Aunt Mae would be delighted to accompany you, if you want her to."

"That would be nice," she agreed.

She paused in the doorway before leaving the kitchen. "Dean?"

He swallowed a mouthful of the leftover cookie. "Mmm?"

"Thank you. For everything."

He smiled. "Good night, Cara."

She nodded and left the room, leaving Dean to wonder what, or who, had put that hopeless, frightened look in her eyes. There was something about her that brought out his protective instincts.

It wasn't a romantic feeling he was developing toward her, he decided, trying to analyze his reactions. More of a big-brotherly attachment, similar to the stronger bond he had with his younger sister.

All in all, he decided, fraternal feelings were much easier to deal with than romantic ones.

HAVING DOWNED the milk and cookies, Dean took a warm shower before bed. He was trying everything he knew, short of pills, to make himself sleepy.

He'd forgotten to take clean underwear into the bathroom with him so he wrapped a towel loosely around his hips and went into his bedroom, where he pulled a pair of soft white cotton briefs out of a bureau drawer. He dropped the towel and bent to step into them.

Something cool and tingly touched his right hip, just below his tan line.

"That really is a cute heart-shaped birthmark," a soft, musical voice said from behind him. "One might almost call it a Valentine mark."

Stumbling and swearing, Dean jerked his underwear into place and turned.

Apparently unfazed by finding him nude, Mary Anna Cameron gave him a melting smile, though it didn't quite reach her eyes. "Hi, Dean."

He leaned heavily against the dresser, his heart still pounding from the start she'd given him—and from the sheer excitement of seeing her again.

He hadn't realized until that moment just how badly he'd missed her. And how afraid he'd been that she wouldn't return.

He really was in big trouble this time.

8

What is life without the radiance of love?
 —Johann Christoph Friedrich von Schiller

"HOW LONG has it been?" Anna asked, her smile fading as she searched his face.

He knew what she was asking. "It's been two weeks since you were here last."

"I see."

"I was beginning to think you weren't coming back." She moved a step closer. "Would you have cared if I hadn't, Dean?"

He held her gaze with his, knowing he shouldn't answer. And yet he heard himself saying, "Yeah. I'd have cared."

Her smile was edged with sadness. She turned away, drifting around the room, touching one thing, then another. "I've been *there*. The waiting place. With Ian. I tried to come back before, but I couldn't, for some reason. I've been here a while today."

"Have you?" He wondered how long she'd been watching him. Had she been there when he'd showered?

"I saw you with that woman. The bleached-blonde who sold you our inn. She asked you out. Women in my day weren't so forward."

"No?" He found it hard to believe Mary Anna Cameron had ever been shy and inhibited.

She laughed softly. "Well, most weren't," she admitted. And then she glanced at him. "You turned her down."

"I wasn't interested."

"Because you still love your ex-wife?"

"No. That was an excuse."

"Oh." She moved to another corner of the room, characteristically restless. "You were alone in the kitchen with the new housekeeper."

"You were there, too?" The thought of her watching him that way, unseen, unheard, bothered him.

She nodded. "I wasn't spying on you," she said as though she'd sensed his discomfort. "I've been trying to catch you alone so we could talk. You seemed too deeply involved in your conversation for me to disturb you then."

"We were just making small talk over a late-night snack." He wasn't explaining himself to her—not exactly, he assured himself. After all, it was none of Anna's business who he talked to. Or went out with. Even if the only woman who really interested him was Anna, herself.

"She seems . . . very nice."

"She is."

Anna had moved closer again, almost within touching range. "Pretty, too. Are you—"

"She's my employee, Anna," Dean said. "That's all."

She sighed, a faint, delicate sound that whispered down his bare spine. "I'm sorry. I didn't mean to pry. I *am* the one who urged you to hire her, after all."

"Yes. But you were right about her. She needed help. And she's a hard worker. If she stays, she'll be a real asset to the inn."

Anna brushed his cheek with her fingertips, that cool, charged touch that was as pleasurable as it was strange. "I shouldn't question you about other women," she said. "You seem very much alone, Dean. It isn't right for you to be lonely."

"I'm—" He had to stop to clear his throat. He hoped Anna didn't notice how her touch affected him. The thin pair of briefs he was wearing provided little cover.

"I'm not lonely," he assured her. "I have my aunt, and my sister. A few new friends. You," he added huskily.

She seemed suddenly fascinated by his bare chest, her hands gliding lightly over his shoulders, down his abdomen to his rib cage. He shivered. It was like being stroked with chilled feathers, leaving him cool and hot at the same time.

"You're so muscular," she murmured. "So strong and tanned. Not soft and pale like . . ." Her voice faded.

Dean frowned. "Like your fiancé?"

Her cheeks took on that glow that resembled a blush. "Jeffrey had very fair skin," she admitted.

"Did you love him?" The question left his mouth before he knew he was going to ask it.

Again, she sighed. "I was very fond of him."

"That was enough for you?"

"It was all I wanted. I was always afraid of passionate love, the kind my mother felt for my father. It seemed so . . . so consuming. So obsessive. I didn't want to give that much of myself to anyone else."

It felt odd, hearing his own feelings put into someone else's words. "I've felt the same way."

"You didn't love your wife?"

"I was fond of her," he replied, turning her own words back to her.

She smiled sadly. "It wasn't enough, was it?"

"No. It wasn't enough."

Her hands still resting on his chest, she looked up at him. "Do you think you'll ever truly love anyone?"

"I don't—"

She tilted her head curiously when he stopped. "You don't what?"

He made a face. "I was going to say I don't believe in that sort of love."

She chuckled. "The way you didn't believe in ghosts?"

"Yeah," he said wryly. "I'm getting tired of eating my words."

"My mother certainly believed in that sort of love. She told us she made a wish the night we were born, a very special, Valentine wish. She wished that neither Ian nor I would leave this earth until we'd found a love like she'd known with our father, and were loved that way in return."

Anna's eyes seemed to darken, with sadness or regret, perhaps. "Obviously, her wish went unfilled. It's too late for that now. If only we can clear our names, then we'll be free to go."

"You seem so sure of that."

"It's the only thing that makes sense to us."

Intensely aware of her nearness, and of the throbbing response of his long-denied body, Dean spoke gruffly. "You're making me reluctant to help you."

Her eyes widened. "Why?"

Very slowly, he touched her face, stroked the marble-cool, unearthly surface of her cheek. "If clearing your name means I'll never see you again, I find it hard to work up enthusiasm for the task."

"That's a very sweet thing to say," she murmured, standing very still beneath his touch.

He shook his head. "Unfortunately, it's the truth. You . . . haunt me, Anna. Even when I can't see you."

She covered his hand with hers, enveloping his warmth in her coolness, emphasizing the differences between them. "Don't," she whispered. "We can't—"

"I know," he muttered, his mouth hovering only inches above hers. "Damn it, I know. But—"

A moment later, she was across the room, her back turned to him. "Have you made any headway in your investigation?" she asked, her voice sounding slightly shaky.

He scrubbed a hand over his face to clear his mind. "No," he answered after a moment. "Not yet. But I am still trying, Anna. As much as I can. I've been asking questions, looking up records, articles . . . I'm trying."

"I believe you."

"I'll talk to the chief of police tomorrow. He's one of Charles Peavy's grandsons. And I still haven't had a chance to talk to Charles's daughter, Margaret, though I don't expect her to be much help."

She nodded briskly. "Sounds like a good plan. I wish—"

"What?"

She looked over her shoulder at him. "I wish I could go with you."

"So do I," he assured her.

"I have to leave now."

He started to reach out for her. He clenched his fist at his side, instead. "You'll be back?"

"I'll be back."

He wished she sounded—and looked—more confident. He wished he knew why she looked so sad tonight. So . . . lost.

Before he could ask her, she was gone.

He lay awake for a long time that night. Hard. Hungry. Hurting.

Knowing he was a fool to even wish things were different.

"YOU'RE BEING very quiet," Ian commented to his sister, breaking the gray silence surrounding them. "Is something bothering you?"

Oh, yes, something was bothering her. And now it was more than the familiar need to find out the truth about what had really happened to place her and her twin in exile in this colorless, joyless place.

Dean had wanted to kiss her. And worse, she'd wanted him to kiss her. Wanted it so badly, she'd ached. She'd even moved toward him, and then she'd realized what a foolish, senseless action that had been.

Dean was a living, breathing, healthy young man with his whole future ahead of him. Anna's life was behind her. She'd never been more keenly aware of her loss.

Maybe she was wrong about Dean being the one to free her. Maybe meeting Dean was as much a punishment for whatever wrongs she'd committed in life as the long years she'd spent in this cold, gray limbo. Perhaps she'd become too complacent in her existence, resigned, if not happy. Ian's companionship had been enough for her...

Until now. Until she'd met Dean. And realized that she had never fully experienced life when she'd lived it. She pictured Jeffrey, and winced. She'd been fond of him, had convinced herself she would be content with his gentle embraces, his deep affection. But now her growing feelings for Dean made her realize that what she'd had with Jeffrey would never have been enough to truly satisfy her.

Wasn't that what Ian had tried repeatedly to tell her?

What cruel twist of fate had forced her to learn that lesson now? What had she done to deserve this? Why had she been allowed to tumble into love for the first time with a man she could never have?

What if it was her destiny to drift out of his reach for the rest of his life, to watch helplessly as he lost interest in a woman whose own life had ended years before his had begun, and turned instead to a woman of flesh and blood? Someone like Cara, so pretty, so sweet, so vulnerable that Anna couldn't blame Dean if he fell for her. Or the other blonde—pushy, but probably pleasant company for a lonely man.

What if Anna had to watch from oblivion as Dean fell in love with someone else, married and started a family of his own?

She could think of no worse punishment, not even an eternity of grayness.

Had she really been so bad? She'd been stubborn, yes, and had occasionally lost her temper. She'd snitched a candy stick from the general store when she was six, but she'd admitted the truth to her mother that very evening. And there'd been those two incidents with Jeffrey—nights when her curiosity and his passion had overcome discretion. She'd known it was wrong, but they *had* planned to marry.

Did she really deserve this? She pictured Dean's face and the aching began again.

"Anna?" Ian repeated, sounding concerned now. "What can I do?"

She forced a smile. "Just be with me," she said, finding solace in her twin's love.

At least she had Ian. She imagined an eternity spent in this place alone, and a shudder ripped through her. Now, *that* would be unbearable, she assured herself. At least she'd been spared that.

"I APPRECIATE your taking the time to see me this afternoon, Mrs. Vandover," Dean said the next afternoon over tea in Margaret Peavy Vandover's elegantly decorated parlor.

"It's a pleasure to see you, Mr. Gates. I understand you have some questions about the decor of the inn? I must tell you that I remember very little about the original furnishings. I was only a child when my father sold the inn."

Dean bit the inside of his lip. Charles had sold the inn in 1950, and Margaret had had a child of her own by that time. The mayor had already admitted to Dean that he remembered seeing the rose gardens when his grandfather owned the place.

He didn't bother to argue with her. "I was hoping you could remember a few details about the gardens," he said instead. "They've been allowed to go wild, and it's no longer possible to tell what was originally planted. Can you remember the names of any of the roses your grandmother planted there?"

"My *step*-grandmother," Margaret corrected him regally. "My father was born of my grandfather's first marriage. My biological grandmother died when my father was very young. His father remarried several years later."

"Of course."

"Still, my mother was fond of the rose gardens. She spent many hours tending them during the years that we lived at the inn. I remember quite a few of the roses that were planted there. Damasks and gallicas, moss roses and lovely, delicate climbers. The wonderful old 'antique' roses. I've planted a few of the same varieties in my own gardens, though of course the modern hybrids are so much easier to raise. I'd be happy to make a list of suggestions for you."

"I'd like that. Thank you."

Margaret nodded, obviously pleased with the opportunity to give her expert advice. "Is there anything else you'd like to ask?"

He'd been waiting for this opening. He'd already talked to the chief of police, only to be told, as Mark had been, that no official police records from 1921 had survived, and that there had never been cause for anyone to doubt Deputy Tagert's accounts of the events of that February night at the inn. Chief Peavy hadn't appreciated Dean's speculation that Peavy's ancestors might have been more involved in the scandal than they'd let on, and he'd made his objections quite clear. He'd all but thrown Dean out of his office, and had ordered him to leave the past alone.

Undaunted, Dean had driven straight to Margaret's house. He managed a convincing chuckle. "I've heard most of the old stories of the inn's history, of course. Seems like everyone in town has taken time to tell me about the ghosts."

Margaret's forehead creased in disapproval. "That nonsense again? Honestly, one would think grown people had better things to talk about."

"It is an interesting story, I suppose, if one believes in that sort of thing."

"Which I do not," Margaret said crisply.

"Nor I," Dean agreed hastily. "What rational adult could possibly believe that ghosts are drifting around, endlessly seeking truth and justice?"

"Exactly. Though I don't know what the search for truth and justice has to do with the Cameron twins."

Dean looked vaguely surprised. "According to some of the locals, Ian and Anna Cameron were innocent of any crimes and murdered because they knew too much. It's said they're seeking to clear their names and avenge their deaths before they leave this world and go on to the next."

"What balderdash! Everyone around here knows better than that. Someone's pulling your leg, Mr. Gates. My father's stepsiblings certainly were guilty, as embarrassing as that is for us. There was never a question otherwise."

"It was fortunate for your grandfather that no one ever questioned him about the convenient timing of the twins' deaths. I suppose his reputation in town was so spotless, there was never any suspicion of whether he was involved in the tragedy."

"Convenient timing?" Margaret repeated stiffly.

"Well, he would have had to turn the inn over to them after that night," Dean reminded her almost apologetically. "As suspicious as everyone is these days, that in itself would have called for a more intense investigation. But things were different back then, I suppose."

"They most certainly were. Citizens did not question the word of a respected officer of the law, nor did they make reckless accusations against a prominent local businessman. If anyone has suggested differently to you, Mr. Gates, I wish you would tell me who it was. I would like to have a word with him about viciously slandering my ancestors."

"Forgive me, Mrs. Vandover. No one has said any-thing about your ancestors. I'm afraid I'm a mystery-novel buff. Always looking for a red herring."

"Perhaps you should turn to more edifying reading, Mr. Gates." Margaret's tone was downright chilly now. "Might I suggest the holy book?"

"I'll keep that in mind. Thank you."

Her eyes were even colder than her voice. For the first time, Dean understood how this woman had managed to completely intimidate so many of the townspeople. There was an almost palpable air of menace about her, enough to take him aback, even though he had no real fear of her.

"I'll have my gardener prepare a list of fine roses for you," she said flatly. "My personal secretary will put it in the mail."

He took her less-than-subtle hint, and stood. "Thank you again for your time, Mrs. Vandover, and for the tea. I hope to restore the inn and the gardens to their former elegance, as they were under your father's care."

She didn't seem mollified.

Dean left her home knowing he hadn't exactly in-gratiated himself with her. If he kept going at this rate, he'd soon have all the Peavy family hating him. And he was still no closer to the truth about what had hap-pened on February 14, 1921 than he'd been when he'd first seen Mary Anna Cameron.

He only hoped he could convince her that he really was trying his best. But, damn it, he was an innkeeper, not a private investigator. Just what the hell did she ex-pect from him?

DEAN GOT a speeding ticket on his way home. He was only going five miles above the posted speed limit, something most rural cops overlooked, in his experience. Not this one.

The officer was fifty pounds overweight, his uniform crumpled and stained. He leaned into the window of Dean's car with a scowl. "You were driving like a bat out of hell, Gates," he said without asking for identification. "We don't appreciate newcomers moving into town and risking the lives of our children with their disregard of our laws."

Startled by the unfairness of the attack, Dean was taken aback for a moment. How did this guy—P. Jones, according to his badge—even know Dean's name? They'd never . . .

Suddenly, he understood. This was Chief Peavy's way of letting him know that life in Destiny could be difficult for someone who deliberately annoyed the Peavy family.

Knowing it wouldn't do any good to argue, he kept his mouth shut and signed the ticket, promising only that he'd watch his speed in the future.

"I'd be more careful about a lot of things if I was you," the officer growled, seemingly satisfied that Dean had been easily cowed.

Dean drove home with a scowl of his own, and a renewed determination to learn the truth, though he still didn't know how.

"Dean, my man, you are definitely one brave—or stupid—son of a gun. Guess you know you got the whole Peavy family calling you a nosy, interferin' Yankee."

Dean winced and shifted the receiver to his other ear. "I know I haven't exactly made myself a family favorite," he admitted. "But, damn it, Mark, why are they so mad? All I did was ask if it was possible the Cameron twins were innocent of the crimes they were rumored to have committed."

"And implied that Gaylon Peavy—and maybe even Charles—were somehow involved with their deaths," Mark reminded him. "Not smart, Gates. I've told you how Margaret feels about the family honor. I'm not sure I've convinced you of her almost obsessive loyalty to her father. Apparently, she adored the ground the guy walked on. She's all but canonized him, and few have the nerve to suggest in her presence that he was anything less than perfect."

"If she's so convinced of the family honor, it shouldn't bother her so badly to answer a few simple questions."

"Yeah , well, she's bothered, all right. In fact, she's downright pissed off."

Dean chuckled at Mark's dry drawl. "Okay, so I didn't approach this in the most diplomatic manner. I'm afraid diplomacy has never been my strong point."

"What next? Going to force the senator into a press conference to ask about his granddaddy's alleged shady dealings?"

Sighing, Dean ran a hand through his hair. "Of course not. Though I thought I might ask the senator a few questions. Maybe he could lead me to legal records of the bootlegging investigation. Surely some still exist, somewhere."

"Trust me, Dean, Senator Gaylon Peavy isn't going to help you look into his family history, no more than Margaret or Charles or Roy are likely to. He's got his political future to protect, you remember. Even a hint of scandal—current or seventy-five years in the past— is more than a career politician is willing to risk."

"Well, hell, what am I supposed to do, then? How can I prove anything if no one's willing to cooperate?" Dean directed the question as much at the empty room as to the man on the other end of the telephone line— just in case Anna was listening.

"I wish you'd tell me why this is so important to you, Dean," Mark said, sounding suddenly serious.

Dean sighed. "I wish I could." *But you'd never believe me.*

"You have to know it seems a little strange, your trying to reopen a seventy-five-year-old local police case."

"I know." *And you'd think it even stranger if you knew the real reason I've become involved in this.*

"And you're not saying another word, are you?"

"No. I'm sorry, there's nothing else to say right now."

Mark conceded, if not graciously, at least resignedly. "You'll call me if you find out anything interesting?"

"You'll be the first."

"Thanks. I guess."

Smiling at Mark's grudging tone, Dean hung up the phone.

He looked around the sitting room. "I hope you're satisfied," he remarked to empty air. "Thanks to you, I'm not exactly scoring popularity points in my new hometown. I'm more likely to get run out of town on a rail."

He turned to find Cara McAlister standing in the doorway, watching him oddly. He cleared his throat. "Er, talking to myself," he muttered.

She nodded. "I was just going to ask if you like baked pork chops," she explained. "I thought I'd make that for dinner this evening."

"Sounds good. I, uh, have to go work outside now."

"I'll call you when dinner's ready."

"Thanks." He didn't quite meet her eyes as he passed her on his way out.

He wondered how Anna would feel when he was dragged out of the inn in a straitjacket, which wasn't such a farfetched image, the way things had been going lately.

ANNA WATCHED Dean leave the sitting room. She'd been watching him for a while, but she'd made no attempt to communicate with him. He looked so tired. She knew he'd been working very hard restoring the inn, and trying to find out the truth for her. He was risking his health, his business, his standing in his adopted community, everything . . . for her.

And he'd asked nothing in return.

Was it any wonder she had fallen in love with him?

He probably wished he had never met her. Would there come a day when he'd throw up his hands and tell her so? If he did, she would have to tell him goodbye. She would have to set him free soon, whether he succeeded in finding out the truth or not. He didn't deserve what she'd put him through these past weeks.

It had never occurred to her that a heart no longer beating could still be broken. Now she realized that it could, indeed.

Her own broke a little more each time she forced herself to leave Dean Gates. It would shatter completely the day she had to tell him goodbye forever.

9

Not Death, but Love.

—Emily Dickinson

FOR THE NEXT TWO DAYS, Dean concentrated on researching Deputy Stanley Tagert. The information was
limited, but a picture emerged of a surly, unpopular
man who'd drifted into law enforcement because of his
need for power. He'd married and fathered three children, only one of whom had stayed in the area after
Tagert died in the hunting accident.

Dean tracked down Tagert's grandson, who owned
a struggling grocery store in a small town less than ten
miles from Destiny. He explained that he'd purchased
the Cameron Inn and was researching its history for his
own curiosity. "I understand your grandfather was the
officer who attempted to arrest the Cameron twins."

Genial and cooperative, Arnold Tagert nodded his
balding head. "Yup. My grandma told us about it. Said
he was a real hero, but he paid the ultimate price for his
dedication to the law."

"What did she mean by that?"

Arnold looked around as though afraid he'd be
overheard, though the few customers shopping in the
store were yards away from the corner where he and
Dean stood. "My grandma never believed the Peavys'
story about my grandfather droppin' his gun and ac-

cidentally shootin' hisself. She says she thinks Gaylon Peavy shot him."

Dean looked properly scandalized, though he wanted to cheer, instead. Finally, he'd found someone who doubted the "official" story. Maybe, at last, he was coming closer to the truth. "Why would she think that?"

"Revenge. She says Gaylon was mad as a hornet at my granddad for shootin' his stepkids, even though my granddad swore they shot first."

Dean frowned, not at all satisfied with that explanation. "But I understood Gaylon was never close to his stepchildren."

Arnold Tagert shrugged. "Around these parts, family loyalty goes a long way. Folks said as how Gaylon promised his second wife, the twins' mother, that he'd look out for 'em as long as he was livin', and he might have thought he'd let 'em down by not protectin' 'em from their own criminal ways."

"That doesn't sound very likely," Dean murmured.

Tagert smiled ruefully. "I know that. But Grandma was never quite right after her husband was killed, you know? And as she got older, she just got more peculiar. She always did hate the Peavys."

Again, that darting look around, as though his grandmother were there to eavesdrop. "My mother had the idea that maybe ol' Granddad had chased after Mary Anna Cameron while he was married to my grandmother. They say Mary Anna was a real knockout."

Dean cleared his throat. "Yeah. That's what I've heard."

"Be that as it may, no one ever took Grandma serious about Gaylon killin' her husband. Far as I know, it was ruled an accident and the case was closed within a few days. Grandma never spoke to a Peavy again, not that it bothered 'em any. But she kept up with 'em, for all that. She seemed to know everything they did. Claimed she was waitin' for justice to assert itself."

Dean was getting desperate. "Mr. Tagert—"

"Arnold."

"Thanks. Arnold, is there anyone still alive who actually knew Gaylon Peavy, or the twins? Anyone who might possibly know a bit more about the scandal than is generally known?"

Tagert frowned and scratched his head. "Ain't no one still alive that I know of. Except maybe ol' Bill Watson."

Dean froze. "Bill Watson?" This was a name he hadn't encountered before.

"His mama used to work at the inn, and she and Bill lived there when he was a boy. They moved to Hot Springs not long after the twins died, but Bill went back to Destiny years later and went to work for the Peavy family. Worked for 'em till he was too old to even do odd jobs, and then they shipped him off to some nursing home. If he's still alive, I guess they're still payin' his bills."

"No one's even mentioned him to me before."

Tagert shrugged. "Not surprisin'. Ol' Bill always was a loner, never had family or many friends to speak of. And it's been years since he left. He'd have to be in his late eighties now, assuming he's still alive. Most folks have probably forgot all about him."

"If he is still alive, it's possible that he would remember the twins. Remember that night, maybe."

Tagert nodded. "Yeah, I guess. Would have stuck in his memory, for sure, even if he was just a kid at the time. Not that I ever heard him mention it while he worked for the Peavys. Nobody ever really understood that situation much, anyway."

"Oh? Why not?"

"Far as anyone could tell, ol' Bill never did much. A little drivin', some gardenin', runnin' errands. But the Peavys kept him on the family payroll for years, then took care of him after he got too old to do anything useful. The Peavys weren't exactly known for their loyalty and generosity—unless it was something they could do real public-like, to make 'em look good, you know?"

Dean nodded to show that he got the point. Bill Watson was sounding more interesting all the time. Was it possible that Watson knew something about the shootings, even though he'd been a mere boy at the time? Or were the Peavys more loyal to longtime employees than the grandson of an embittered widow had been led to believe?

Whichever the case, Dean wanted to talk to Watson. "You don't know which nursing home he's in?"

"No, 'fraid not, though I think it was somewhere in Little Rock."

Impatient to be away, Dean thanked Tagert for his time.

"Oh, yeah, sure. Listen, good luck with the inn, you hear? I always thought it was a purty place despite all the bad luck that seemed to surround it—not that I expect anything like that for you, of course," Tagert added quickly.

Dean smiled wryly. "I hope you're right. Bring the wife for dinner some night when the dining room's open. Your meal will be on the house."

Tagert seemed delighted by the generous offer.

DEAN CALLED Mark from his car phone. "Have you heard the name Bill Watson?" he asked, barely taking time to identify himself.

"Watson, er, wasn't he once a handyman for the Peavy family?"

"That's the one. Why didn't you mention him before?"

"I forgot," Mark confessed.

Dean scowled, but managed to keep his irritation in check. "What do you know about him?"

"Not much. His name came up when I started doing my research into the shoot-out. Someone remembered that he'd lived in the inn at that time. But I was told that old Bill is senile and hardly remembers his own name, much less anything about the Cameron family. He left Destiny in his late teens, came back fifteen years later and went to work for Margaret's father, Charles. Stayed on the family payroll until he got too old and then they put him in a nursing home somewhere."

"You don't know where?"

"No. Before I could start looking for him, I got busy with the problems at the paper. He completely slipped my mind after that."

"Then I guess I'll just have to start calling nursing homes. I've been told to try the ones in Little Rock first."

"You really think this could be a lead? What if the old man really *is* senile?"

"It's worth a shot," Dean said tiredly. "It's not as though I have that many more leads to pursue."

He wondered when he would see Anna again to discuss his progress. And then he chided himself for making excuses, when the truth was that he just wanted to see Anna again, period.

Mae was working in the newly restored lobby when Dean walked in. She looked up from the corner where she was sweeping up wood shavings left by the finish carpenters. "Back from another of your mysterious outings?" she asked with a faint smile.

Dean knew his aunt was growing worried about him. He was well aware that his behavior during the past few weeks hadn't exactly been typical, for him. But then, he would be surprised if he could act completely normal, considering that everything he'd once believed had so radically changed.

He'd met a ghost, and was trying to solve her murder. And he was in danger of falling very hard for a woman who'd been dead seventy-five years.

How *could* he behave as though nothing was different?

"Just getting to know our new neighbors," he assured his aunt with a vague smile of his own.

"Making friends or new enemies?"

He winced. "Er, what do you mean?"

"I've heard that you aren't making yourself overly popular with the Peavys. What's going on, Dean? Why are you asking so many questions about the death of the Cameron twins?"

He tried to look surprised. "Weren't you the one who encouraged me to find out more about the history of the inn? Both you and Bailey said I should have answers ready if any of our guests ask about the Cameron legend."

"Well, yes, but aren't you carrying it a little too far? A woman at the supermarket whispered to me that you practically accused Margaret Vandover's late grandfather of murdering his stepchildren. Margaret was highly offended."

Gossip really did get around fast in this town, Dean thought wryly. He was surprised that Margaret had repeated Dean's suspicions, as protective as she was of the family name. Or was she warning the townspeople not to cooperate with him in his quixotic quest for the truth?

"Dean?" His aunt stepped closer and rested a hand on his arm. "Darling, is there something you want to talk to me about? Something that can help me understand the way you've been acting lately? Distant. Distracted. Talking to yourself—you've never done that before. What's bothering you, dear? Why can't you talk to me about it?"

He felt like a first-class, A-number-one jerk. He put his arms around his aunt and gave her a bracing hug.

"Aunt Mae, please. Don't worry about me. You know how I am when I get interested in something. It consumes me for a while. That's what made me such a workaholic before. We've even talked about how I'd probably do the same thing with the inn that I've done with my other jobs."

She nodded against his shoulder. "It's what makes you so successful at whatever you do," she admitted. "You give it everything you have. But this ghost story—"

"Part of the inn's history," he reminded her. "A very notorious part. If there's any chance the legend will affect my success, one way or another, I want to be prepared."

"I suppose that makes sense," Mae conceded doubtfully.

"Sure it does. I just want to ask a few more questions, find out everything I can, and then I'll forget all about it and concentrate on running the best inn and restaurant in all of central Arkansas," he assured her.

Not that he expected to forget about Mary Anna Cameron. Ever. But he saw no need to mention that particular obsession.

His aunt was worried enough.

"As a matter of fact," he said, setting her gently away from him, "I'm going to concentrate on nothing but the inn for the rest of the day. It's time I start pulling down those decrepit outbuildings before someone gets hurt."

"I wish you'd let the workers you hired take care of that," Mae fretted. "You're the one who could get hurt."

"I'll be careful. Remember how we discussed that the more work we do ourselves, the more we can save on the total cost of renovations?"

"You aren't running low on funds, are you, Dean?"

He made a face. "It's taking everything I have," he admitted. "But there's enough left to finish. Let's just hope business is brisk enough to keep us in beans and rice for the first year of business."

She smiled. "I'm sure you're exaggerating, but I do hope business goes well. Do try not to antagonize all the locals, will you, dear?"

"I'll try, Aunt Mae," he agreed, though he couldn't promise he wouldn't further infuriate the Peavys. Not if it meant clearing the twins' names.

LATER THAT AFTERNOON, Dean was working in a small, eight-by-ten shed that might once have been used for storing gardening equipment. Though not in as poor shape as the shack at the end of the garden path, this building, too, had been allowed to fall into disrepair. Dean and the building contractor had agreed that it would be easier to tear it down and build a new garden shed than to try to restore this one.

It wasn't a difficult job. Basically, the building consisted of four wooden walls and a rough wooden floor. A window had been cut into one side wall, the glass long gone. A round vent hole, covered with a battered shutter, had been cut high into the back wall. The door was a simple, hinged sheet of plywood with a rusty padlock that no longer closed. Dean took that down first, and then started ripping off the rusted tin that covered the low, flat plywood roof.

He stopped only once during the next hour, when his aunt summoned him inside for a telephone call. The telephone discussion with a plumbing-supplies distributor took some twenty minutes. Afterward, Dean went into the kitchen for a drink of water, then returned to the shed, hoping to get at least halfway through the job that afternoon.

When the tin from the roof was stacked in a pile to be taken to a salvage yard, he moved inside the shed to decide where to start next. He sneezed as dust hovered in the air around him, disturbed by his work.

A hairy black spider scuttled across the toe of his work boot; he left it alone. His sister had an almost phobic fear of spiders, but Dean had never shared her aversion to them. Nor had he ever ridiculed her because of it.

The thought of Bailey made him wistful. He missed her. He wished she were here with him now.

Bailey was the only person he knew who might understand if he told her about Anna. It wasn't that Bailey had ever expressed an interest in the supernatural, but she had always believed Dean. Always.

He was almost tempted to call her and tell her everything. But something held him back. Maybe he was afraid that this time, Bailey would be as skeptical as he knew everyone else would be should he reveal his relationship with the long-dead Mary Anna Cameron.

Letting out a long, frustrated breath, he glanced upward. He noticed that someone had laid planks halfway across the open rafters, creating a loft of sorts. Had someone stored bags of fertilizer or mulch there? It seemed a logical supposition.

Just then, he heard a rustling noise from one corner of the makeshift loft. Grimacing, he glanced at the retreating spider and wondered if mice had also made their winter home in this shed. He didn't mind the bugs so much, but mice were a different story.

Once, while Dean was exploring a horse-loving friend's barn as a teenager, a mouse had run up the leg of his jeans. Dean had come out of those jeans right in front of three teenage girls and two male school pals, catching the mouse just as it reached sensitive territory. Since that incident, Dean had fought an unmanly temptation to jump on a chair every time someone even said the word *mouse.*

He turned his back to the loft. Maybe he'd go back to work outside. By the time he'd removed most of the walls, any creature residing in the shack should have taken the hint and departed.

A scraping sound from above him caught his attention just as Mary Anna appeared in front of him. "Dean!" she cried, her voice distant and frantic. *"Move!"*

Instinctively, he ducked and threw himself forward. Something hard and heavy hit him across the right shoulder. Something so heavy he collapsed beneath it.

Had he not been moving forward, it would have hit him squarely on the head.

Pain exploded from his injured shoulder and radiated through the rest of him as he landed jarringly on the dirty wooden floor. Whatever it was that had hit him now held him pinned. He was dimly conscious of a creaking noise from above him, and then a heavy thud that sounded as though it had come from just outside the shed. He hurt too much to try to figure out what he'd heard.

"Dean. Oh, Dean, are you all right?" Anna hovered beside him, wringing her pale hands. "Can you move?"

He groaned and shifted, the movement sending bursts of pain from his shoulder to the back of his head. "No," he gasped. "It's too heavy."

He tried to see what was holding him down, but he couldn't turn his head that far. Whatever it was, it felt as though it weighed a ton.

His right arm was numb, and he couldn't move his fingers. Something warm and wet trickled beneath his torn sweatshirt and dripped onto the boards beneath him.

"Anna," he muttered, his vision blurring. "Help me."

"I can't," she said, her voice sounding like a sob. "I tried to move it, but I can't."

His mind was spinning now, the pain from his arm and shoulder almost overwhelming. It took all his strength to form words. "Can you—can you bring someone to me?"

"I'll try," she promised. "Oh, Dean, I'm so sorry."

He rested his forehead on the floor, oblivious now to the dirt and the roughness of the wood. "Get—help," he muttered. And then he closed his eyes and allowed the darkness to engulf him.

HE DIDN'T KNOW how much time passed before his aunt came to him. As he drifted in a haze of pain and confusion, it could have been minutes or hours for all he knew.

"Dean! Oh, my God, what happened to you?" Mae knelt beside him, her hands on his face, at his throat. "Dear, can you talk to me?"

He moaned. "I can't—get up," he managed to say.

Mae ran to the door of the shed. "Cara," she called loudly. "Call 911. And then come out here and help me. Hurry! Dean's hurt!"

Relieved that help had arrived, Dean tried to fight the darkness that threatened to take him again. He wanted to stay conscious, wanted to know just how badly he was hurt.

He groaned when his aunt cautiously shifted the object lying across him. Every movement made his right arm and shoulder throb as though someone were kicking him.

"I'm sorry, dear. Maybe Cara and I can lift it quickly without hurting you too much."

"Be careful," Dean muttered. "It's—heavy."

"I know. But I think the two of us can manage it."

"What—what is it?"

"I don't know. It looks like an old table. A potting bench, maybe. The top is wood, but the frame is metal. Oh, Dean, you're bleeding. You have a bad cut on your right arm, all the way up to your shoulder."

He'd already guessed that. He hoped nothing was broken, nothing vital severed.

He could only imagine what shape he would be in if the bench had hit his head. If Anna hadn't—

He tried to lift his head. He didn't see Anna anywhere. "Aunt Mae . . . how did you—"

"Don't talk, Dean. You need to conserve your strength."

He stubbornly persisted. "How did you know I was in trouble?"

She looked perplexed for a moment. "I don't know, exactly. I was working in the lobby, and suddenly I had a very strong, almost panicky feeling that I should check on you. I'm just glad I paid attention to my feelings . . . Oh, Cara, there you are. Let's try to get this off of him, shall we?"

Cara was already kneeling at Dean's other side. "Should we try to move it? We could injure him more seriously. Help is on the way."

"Get it off, if you can," Dean muttered. "It's too damned heavy. I can hardly breathe." He was starting to feel distinctly claustrophobic.

Though Cara still seemed inclined to believe it would be better to wait, she allowed herself to be persuaded. She and Mae took hold of opposite sides of the bench, counted to three and then shifted it off Dean's back in one smooth, forceful effort. They dropped the bench at Dean's left side, then shoved it to one corner of the cramped shed and out of the way.

Dean's relief at having the weight removed was overwhelmed by a fresh wave of pain that crashed through him. He finally surrendered to it, and to the oblivion that followed. His last clear thought was of Anna, and of the fear and hopelessness in her eyes when she'd knelt beside him.

FORTUNATELY, there were no broken bones, though the jagged cut that ran from Dean's right shoulder almost down to his elbow required quite a few stitches. He left the emergency room of the small county hospital with his arm in a sling, his hip stinging from a tetanus shot, a bottle of painkillers in his left hand and the doctor's long list of instructions still ringing in his ears.

His ruined sweatshirt had been cut away; his bare chest was covered only by the bandages and the woolen jacket he kept in his car.

His aunt hovered at his right side, guiding him as though he were a feeble old codger, he thought ruefully. Cara and Casey trailed behind them, their faces creased in almost identical expressions of concern. Cara drove Dean's car, with Casey riding in the front passenger seat so that Dean and his aunt could share the back seat.

"I'll be fine, Aunt Mae," he assured her for at least the hundredth time. "It hurts like he—heck," he hastily amended with a glance at Casey, "but it's nothing permanent. You heard the doctor."

"I heard him say how very lucky you were that the bench didn't break your back or split your skull," Mae retorted, clearly still badly shaken from the ordeal.

Dean nodded meaningfully in the direction of the little girl who was listening so intently in the front seat. "None of that happened, Aunt Mae," he said firmly, "it was just an unfortunate accident, and I'll be fine. But I want all of you to stay away from those old buildings, you hear? Now we know just how dangerous they are. Right, Casey?"

She nodded. "I won't go near them, Mr. Gates," she said fervently.

"Good girl."

"Now you'll have to hire someone to take them down," Mae said with obvious satisfaction. "The doctor said you shouldn't do any strenuous work with that arm for several weeks after the stitches are removed."

"I'll talk to the contractor tomorrow," Dean conceded.

He rested his throbbing head against the back of his seat. Man, he was tired. And he ached all over. He knew that when all the painkillers wore off, his arm was going to hurt like a real son of a bitch. And he hated taking pills.

He wanted to know what had happened. How that potting bench had gotten into the loft when he knew damned well it hadn't been there earlier. What had made those scraping sounds he'd heard just before the bench had crashed down on him and what had caused that thud moments later?

Maybe Anna would have some answers for him.

MAE AND CARA insisted that Dean go straight to bed when they got home, though Dean protested that he was perfectly capable of sitting in a chair. They wouldn't hear of it, and once he was lying down, he was secretly relieved he'd given in.

They offered to bring him dinner on a tray, but he refused. His stomach was still too unsettled for solid food. He compromised by drinking a cup of bouillon. Aunt Mae didn't leave him alone until she'd watched him take the painkillers the doctor had prescribed for him. Then, promising to check on him frequently, she tiptoed out of the room, turning out the overhead light and leaving only the dimmed bedside lamp to softly illuminate the room.

Dean waited for Anna to appear—or at least he tried to wait. Pain, exhaustion and the strong medication were combining to make him sleepy. It was all he could do to hold his eyes open, scanning the shadowy corners of his bedroom for any sign of his dark-eyed ghost.

Sleep won out. Dean closed his eyes and settled into the pillows with a deep sigh. He would talk to Anna later.

He slept heavily. He roused a time or two when his aunt came in to check on him, and he assured her each time that he was fine and that he'd call out if he needed her during the night. Cara tiptoed in once, shyly feeling his forehead and then insisting that he take another pill. He murmured a grudging thank-you and a firm good-night, then closed his eyes and went back to sleep.

His dreams were vivid, disturbing. Flashes of pain and that sense of helplessness he'd felt when he'd been pinned beneath the potting bench, alone in the shed, unable to move, not knowing whether anyone would find him before he bled to death. Memories of Anna, leaning over him, her voice broken as she'd cried out her inability to help him. Echoes of that shuffling, creaking noise above him just before Dean's world had exploded in pain.

And then he dreamed of Anna. Her cool hands against his face. Her lips moving beneath his.

He shifted against the sheets, and his body throbbed with arousal now in addition to the underlying pain.

"Anna," he murmured, holding her close in his dreams. "Anna."

"Dean," she whispered in return, her voice that musical, far-off litany that had haunted him, waking and dreaming.

She caressed his face, and then moved her hands to stroke his shoulders, his bare chest, his stomach. He stirred beneath her touch, groaning when his injured arm protested the movement.

"Lie still," she murmured, gently holding him down. "I need to know you're all right."

"I'm okay," he muttered, his tongue thick with sleep and the effects of medication. "Just—my arm."

She pressed a kiss on his shoulder, just above the thick bandage. And then on the side of his throat. And on his chest, just above his right nipple.

Each kiss was like a tiny electrical charge. Not unpleasant. Tingly.

He'd kicked off the thin sheet that had covered him, leaving him clad only in his briefs. Anna explored every exposed inch of him, finding every scratch, every bruise, anointing them with those fleeting, stimulating kisses. He could almost feel the energy stirring within him, as though she was transferring her own vibrancy to him.

She left an all new kind of pain in her wake.

"Anna," he said from between his teeth. "I want you."

Very lightly, she touched the swollen ridge beneath his briefs. "I know," she murmured, her tone sad. "I wish—"

He reached for her. Then cursed when the movement made his arm scream in protest.

"Lie still," she said quickly, touching his arm, encouraging him to rest it on the pillow his aunt had arranged beneath him. "You mustn't strain your arm."

He fought the encroaching drugged sleepiness. "Don't go," he muttered, struggling to focus, still unsure of whether he was awake or asleep. "Stay with me."

She laid her fingertips against his lips. "I can't. I have to go now."

"No. I—I need—"

"Sleep," she whispered. "You need sleep."

"Anna—"

He felt something brush his lips again. He thought perhaps she'd kissed him.

Before he could respond, she was gone.

He groaned and covered his eyes with his good arm.

God help him, he'd fallen in love. With a ghost. Perhaps that was only fitting for a man who had never believed in either.

10

The course of true love never did run smooth.
—William Shakespeare

DEAN WAS in the sitting room the next afternoon, settled into an easy chair with a cup of tea and the newspaper, both of which he tried to juggle with his left hand. He wasn't doing very well at it.

He couldn't really concentrate on the newspaper, anyway. All he could think about was Anna.

Had she really come to him during the night, or had he dreamed her? Had she kissed him, touched him, or was it only the medication that had made his fantasies seem so real?

Was he really in love with her, or was this only desire, fueled by a long spell of celibacy? And if he did love her, what the hell was he supposed to do about it?

The telephone rang. He ignored it. It was answered by someone else in the house, but a moment later Casey appeared in the doorway.

"It's for you, Mr. Gates," she said, motioning toward the extension on the cherry-wood table at his left side.

"Thank you, Casey."

She nodded and disappeared.

Folding the newspaper in his lap, Dean lifted the receiver. "Gates."

"I hear you've done battle with a potting bench. And you lost."

"Yeah, something like that," Dean answered wryly, recognizing Mark's voice.

"Seriously, Dean, are you all right? The local grapevine has you all but dead. One gossip-loving matron told me your arm had been amputated, though Cara assured me it wasn't quite that serious."

"Not nearly that serious." Dean had noticed how Mark's voice softened when he'd said Cara's name. "You talked to Cara?"

"Briefly," Mark said, frustration in his tone. "She took only enough time to assure me that you weren't mortally injured before she sent Casey off to call you to the phone. I wish I knew what that woman has against me."

"I doubt that it's you, personally. I don't think she wants to get too deeply involved with *anyone*."

"She just needs time to get used to the idea, that's all," Mark said stubbornly. And then he changed the subject before Dean could comment. "Tell me what happened. All I know is that something fell on you and ripped your arm open."

"I was tearing down the garden shed, when an old metal-framed potting bench fell from a loft above me. Had I not ducked at the last moment, my injuries would probably be worse than they are," Dean explained, thinking that Anna could well have saved his life with her warning.

"What was a heavy potting bench doing up in the loft?"

"I wish I knew. It wasn't there a couple of hours earlier."

There was a pause at the other end of the line. "You're sure of that?"

"I'm sure of that," Dean repeated grimly. "I looked that whole shed over before I started working on it. I had noticed the bench outside, behind the building."

"I saw a man lift it into the loft," Anna said quietly, appearing suddenly at Dean's side. "The same man who pushed it onto you."

Dean straightened abruptly, staring at her. "Who?" he mouthed, frustrated by knowing Mark would hear him if he spoke aloud.

She shrugged. "A man of maybe thirty years old. His clothes were shabby and his hair was too long. Both were dirty. He'd been watching you, and when you went inside to take your phone call, he moved the bench to the loft. He waited there for you to return. After he . . . attacked you, he climbed out the round window and jumped to the ground. I don't know where he went after that. I was worried about you."

Except for that one break, she spoke flatly, mechanically. Her eyes held all the turbulent feelings she'd tried to repress.

"Dean?" Mark prodded after a moment. "What—"

"Someone pushed the bench onto me," Dean cut in, his own voice hardened by anger. "It was deliberate, Mark."

"How do you know that?"

"I, er, caught a glimpse of him, up in the loft. Before I could react, I was pinned under the bench and he was gone."

"But Cara said it was an accident. She didn't mention a deliberate attack."

"She doesn't know. You're the only one I've told."

"For crying out loud, Dean, why? Why didn't you call the cops? Chief Peavy would—oh, hell."

Dean waited for Mark to reach the obvious conclusion.

It didn't take long.

"The Peavys," Dean confirmed. "Maybe I've gotten too close to the truth for comfort."

"I'm coming over. We're going to talk about this."

"Okay, sure. Come on over. I'll tell you what little I know. But don't expect any more proof than I've offered you before. I still don't have it. Not yet."

"I'll be there in twenty minutes."

Still looking at Anna, Dean hung up the phone. "Tell me again," he ordered her. "From the beginning."

She repeated what she'd said earlier. She'd seen the man skulking behind bushes, watching Dean work. She'd watched him set up the attack.

"I tried to warn you," she said, wringing her hands and avoiding his eyes. "I could see he was up to no good, and I wanted to let you know. But I...couldn't."

"Why not?" he asked, keeping his voice gentle. He could sense the extent of her distress.

"I don't know. Maybe I panicked. Maybe I was trying too hard. But I—" Her voice cracked. He could hardly hear her next words. "He almost killed you."

Dean pushed himself carefully out of the chair. "But he didn't, Anna. Thanks to you. It was because of your warning that I wasn't standing directly beneath the bench when it fell."

Looking away from him, she crossed her arms over her chest, as though she were chilled. Dean wondered if she felt cold. Or pain. Or need.

"I was so afraid for you," she whispered. "I felt so helpless. And then you were lying there, bleeding, with that big bench on top of you, and I couldn't even move it. I tried, but my hand passed through it. As though— as though I wasn't even there."

Dean took a step closer to her. "Anna, it's okay. You did your best. You managed to warn me, and then somehow you got help. I'm very grateful to you."

She looked at him then, and her eyes were so tortured that his throat tightened. He had his answer now. She *could* feel pain. And it was tearing him apart.

"It was like I wasn't even there," she repeated in a whisper. "As though I was . . . dead."

The word hung heavily between them.

Dean forced her name past a painful lump in his throat. "Anna."

She covered her face with her hands. "No," she whispered. "Don't say anything yet."

He gave her a moment, then tried again. "Anna."

Her composure regained, she lowered her hands. "You think you were attacked because you've been investigating our deaths."

It wasn't a question, but Dean nodded. "That's a possibility. One of several, of course."

"I want you to stop. Now. No more questions, no more probing. Run our—your inn. Forget you ever saw me."

He lifted a hand to her marble-cold cheek. "You don't really think I can do that, do you?"

She covered his hand with her own. "You have no choice. I don't want you hurt, Dean. I couldn't bear it if anything happened to you because of me."

He shook his head. "Nothing's going to happen to me."

She looked pointedly at his bandages, at the sling supporting his right arm. "Something already did. And next time, it could be worse."

"There won't be a next time."

She moved away from him, her gestures sharp, exasperated. "How do you *know* that?"

"I'll be careful."

"The way Ian and I were careful?" she said hotly.

"You weren't expecting anything to happen," he retorted. "I am. And next time, if there is a next time, I won't be caught unaware."

"Dean, please—"

"This isn't open to discussion, Anna. I promised to clear your name, and your brother's. And if there's any way I can do so, I will."

She looked up at him through her lashes. "You're so anxious to be rid of me?"

It was like a blow to his chest, knowing his success would mean that she would leave him. "I don't ever want to be rid of you," he said huskily.

She searched his face with widened eyes. "Dean—"

"Do you need me to spell it out for you?"

"No," she whispered, looking away. "It would be better if you didn't. This . . . this can't be."

"You think I don't know that? It doesn't seem to make any difference."

"I don't want you hurt." Her voice was thick. "By me, or by anyone else."

"You let me worry about myself," he advised her. "You think about Ian, and that cold, gray waiting area you both hate so much. Think—think about seeing your mother again."

She seemed to catch her breath; Dean didn't even want to think about whether she breathed at all.

"I have to go," she said quietly.

"I know."

But she'd be back. At least a few more times.

Their gazes locked for a long, silent moment. Dean read his own emotions in her eyes.

And then he was alone.

He muttered a curse and scrubbed his left hand wearily over his face.

"Dean?" His aunt appeared in the doorway, watching him with loving, worried eyes. "Are you in pain, dear?"

"Yeah," he groaned. "It hurts, Aunt Mae. It hurts like hell."

He wasn't talking about his arm. Since she didn't know that, she fussed over him, insisting that he sit down and put his feet up. He refused another painkiller, but accepted a fresh cup of tea, which she hurried to get for him.

Dean leaned his head against the back of his chair and closed his eyes, wondering what he had ever done to deserve this.

"I'VE GOT to talk to Bill Watson," Dean said flatly that afternoon after he'd told Mark all his suspicions about the murders of the Cameron twins and the bootlegger named Buck Felcher. He'd added his theory that Gaylon Peavy had then killed Stanley Tagert, the only surviving witness to the shoot-out.

Mark had heard him out with an open mind, though he couldn't quite hide his skepticism. "It all sounds like the plot of a bad gangster movie," he said when Dean had finished.

"I know," Dean agreed. "But this really happened."

"And you think Bill Watson knows something incriminating about the Peavys? Even if he's coherent enough to tell you?"

"I think he might. Tagert's grandson made it clear that he thought Watson had something on the Peavys. Why else would they have supported him all those years for doing so very little in return?"

"Do you know where Watson is?"

"No. But I'll find him."

"I'm going with you when you talk to him."

In response to Dean's lifted eyebrow, Mark nodded toward the bandages. "You're in no shape to drive yourself for a while. And if there is any danger in your pursuit of this crazy quest, you need someone around who's on your side."

Dean smiled, touched. "Thanks, Mark. I appreciate it."

"Just one thing. If Watson denies any knowledge of this, will you drop it?"

"I don't know that I have any other choice," Dean said grimly. "He's my last resort. As far as I can tell, I have no other way of proving my suspicions unless he knows something."

"And after we talk to him, you'll tell me what put this bee in your bonnet in the first place?"

Dean agreed.

He'd have to think of something to placate the too-perceptive journalist. He wasn't sure their friendship would survive the ghost story Dean would have to tell if he couldn't come up with a more plausible tale.

TWO DAYS LATER, on February 13, Dean was in the passenger seat of Mark's sports car, headed for a nursing home in Little Rock.

Dean hadn't seen Anna since she'd left him in the sitting room. He suspected that this time she was deliberately staying away from him. He saw the wisdom in her actions, but, God, he missed her.

How would he stand it when she was gone forever?

"You're very quiet today," Mark commented, glancing at Dean from behind the wheel. "Arm bothering you?"

Dean drew his gaze away from the side window, through which he'd been staring at nothing. "No," he said. "Just thinking."

"Nothing else has happened since your accident, has it?"

"No. A few people stopped by to make sure I was okay, which I thought was very nice, but no word from the Peavys, if that's what you're asking. If they did hire someone to warn me off, they probably assume their message was received."

Mark changed the subject. "I hear Cara's enrolling Casey in school next week."

"Did Cara tell you?"

"No. I ran into the school principal at the café. She told me."

"Ah, yes, the Destiny grapevine."

Mark sighed. "Cara doesn't tell me anything. Every time she sees me, she all but runs in the opposite direction. You know, if she keeps this up, I'm liable to get my feelings hurt."

Dean smiled. "Give her time, Mark."

Mark shook his head. "You probably think I'm nuts, but—well, hell, this has never happened to me before. I mean, I took one look at her and, pow! It's weird, but I haven't been able to stop thinking about her since, even though she's done everything but wear a sign that tells me she's not interested. Anything like that ever happen to you?"

Dean thought of Anna. The way she haunted his thoughts. The way his chest tightened every time he was close to her—along with other vital parts of his anatomy. The constant need to see her, hear her. Touch her. Even though he knew it couldn't be.

"Yeah," he muttered. "Something like that."

Mark glanced sideways again. "Your ex-wife?"

"No."

"Someone since?"

"Yeah."

"Anything come of it?"

Dean exhaled. "We have ... irreconcilable differences."

"I'm not trying to pry, you understand. Just thought maybe you'd have some words of advice to offer. I mean, not only have I never been married before, I've never even been in love before. It just hasn't happened for me. Damn it, I don't even know if this *is*—"

Mark broke off, his cheeks suspiciously flushed. "Hell," he muttered. "I sound like a schoolkid."

Dean chuckled faintly. "You sound like a bewildered male. And trust me, pal, I know the feeling."

He couldn't help thinking how ironic it was that Mark thought Cara was unattainable. At least *she* was alive.

But dark humor didn't help. Telling himself how pointless it was didn't help. Nothing helped.

Dean was in love with Anna—whoever, whatever, *when*ever she was. And it wasn't something he was ever going to get over.

BILL WATSON was eighty-five years old, gravely ill and confined to a bed for the past three years. His mind, they were told, was as sharp as it had ever been, his disposition as sour.

"So the Peavys lied about his mental condition, too," Mark muttered. "Looks like they have something to hide, after all."

"And that Bill Watson knows something," Dean agreed.

"Frankly, I'm surprised he agreed to see you," the male nurse told Dean and Mark as he escorted them to Watson's room. "He doesn't usually want company."

After locating Watson by calling nearly every nursing home in central Arkansas, Dean had sent word that he and Mark were interested in the history of the Cameron Inn, and anything Watson could tell them about his time there. Watson had responded almost immediately with an agreement to talk to them, on the condition that they make it soon. They had wasted no time coming to see him.

"How sick is he?" Dean asked the nurse as they reached Watson's door.

The man's expression spoke volumes. "Another six weeks. Maybe," he said pessimistically. "I don't know how he's held on this long, to be honest."

Watson lay in a metal-framed hospital bed, his bald head propped on pillows, his withered body barely a lump beneath the sheets. "Which one of you bought the inn?" he barked wheezily before Dean and Mark could even introduce themselves.

Dean stepped closer to the bed. "I did. I'm Dean Gates."

"You seen the ghosts?"

"I—er—"

"I saw 'em. Twenty years ago, on Valentine's Day. Like to scared me into a heart attack right then. I ain't been the same since. A year later, they stuck me here." Watson sounded angry.

Dean sank into the chrome-legged chair beside the bed, needing its support. "You . . . saw them? Both of them?" He wondered why Anna had never mentioned it.

Watson nodded, his bleary gaze distant. "Don't know why I went out to the inn. Some kind of ignorant impulse. It was nighttime. 'Bout the same time of night the twins was killed. And there they was, standing by the old caretaker's shack, looking at me and shaking their heads."

Mark cleared his throat and gave Dean a look that said he thought the nurse had been exaggerating about Watson's clarity of mind.

Dean knew better. "Did they speak to you?" he asked, ignoring Mark's startled look.

"No. I didn't give 'em a chance. I got the hell out of there." Watson gave a sickly smile that showed his toothlessness. The smile faded almost immediately. "Didn't matter. I know what they would have said if they'd known who I was."

Dean leaned closer. "And what was that?"

The old man's eyes focused inward. "They would've wanted me to tell the truth."

Dean's heart began to pound. "The truth?"

His gaze sharpening, Watson looked at Mark. "You the reporter fella'?"

Mark stepped forward. "Yes, sir."

"Bring your notebook?"

Pulling a battered notebook out of his back pocket, Mark nodded. "I never leave home without it," he quipped.

"Get out your pen. And write fast. I ain't telling this more than once, and I don't want a bunch of questions."

Mark looked at Dean, then flipped open the notebook. "I'm ready."

Watson turned back to Dean, as though sensing who had the most interest in what he had to say. "I been blackmailing the Peavy family for almost sixty years. They treated me like dirt the whole time. Just like Gaylon Peavy—the first one—treated my ma. I put up with it 'cause they always paid me regular, but now it don't matter. I ain't going to be around much longer, and before I go, I got a few scores to settle."

Dean didn't risk asking questions that might have annoyed the old man. He merely nodded. And waited, tense with anticipation.

Watson wheezed, coughed and then cleared his throat. "My mama started working for Gaylon and Amelia Peavy when the twins was just little 'uns. I was born a few years later. My dad run off, and Mama had to keep working to support me, but Miz Amelia promised her we'd always have a home there at the inn. Miz Amelia was like that," he added meditatively. "A real nice lady, from what my mama said. I don't remember her, myself."

"And the twins?" Dean dared. "Do you remember them?"

"Sure do. My mama thought the sun rose and fell on those two. She didn't much like Gaylon, but she loved them twins like her own, 'specially after their ma died. Ian promised her that when he ran the inn, she'd always have a home there, just like his ma promised before him. Ian always had a temper, but he never lost it with Ma. He was real good to her. Didn't treat her like hired help, like some of them others did."

"And Anna?" Dean couldn't help asking. "Was she nice to your mother?"

Watson's eyebrow rose in surprise. "You called her Anna," he commented. "That's what her brother and her close friends called her. Everyone else called her by her full name, Mary Anna. But, yeah, she was nice to everyone. She used to bring me back candy when she went to town. She was one beautiful woman. For a while, all the boys in town chased after her. Most of 'em gave up when they saw they couldn't ever separate her from her brother.

"Ian—he was different from the others. He had that funny name his Brit father give him, and a bunch of big dreams about owning a whole chain of inns. Seemed like all he cared about was the inn and his sister."

"Was that why he turned to bootlegging?" Mark asked. "To raise money for his dreams?"

Watson snorted. "Ian Cameron never ran a bottle of hooch in his life. He was a hotheaded son of a gun, but he was honest."

"You were ten years old when he died," Mark said. "How do you know what he was like?"

"My mama knew," Watson insisted. "She'd have knowed if he was messing around with criminals. He wasn't. Besides, I *saw* what happened to him. I know he didn't do what Tagert said."

"You witnessed his murder?" Dean asked, startled. "You know who killed him?"

Watson's eyes gleamed with a sick satisfaction that made Dean's stomach clench. "I know. I've always known."

"Why didn't you tell anyone?"

"'Cause he told me he'd kill me if I did. Me and my ma. I was ten years old. I believed him. He fired my ma a short time later, and she got a job at the Arlington Hotel in Hot Springs. I ran off when I was fifteen— didn't want to be a burden to her anymore. I was going to make enough money to take care of her, so she didn't have to work so hard. She died before I was old enough to get a decent job that would've taken care of both of us."

The bitterness was still there, after all these years. Dean bit back the words of sympathy he knew wouldn't be appreciated. "Who killed the twins, Bill?" he asked, instead. "Was it Gaylon Peavy?"

Mark's pen stilled over the notebook.

"Wasn't Gaylon," Watson answered flatly. "It was his son, Charles. Charles was the bootlegger. He never cared squat about that inn. Money, that was all he ever cared about. He had quite an operation going, him and Buck Felcher—and Stanley Tagert. Tagert was in on it from the first."

"You're sure about this?" Mark asked, looking a bit worried.

Watson scowled. "Of course I'm sure. I been collecting money on that memory for sixty years. Think they'd have paid me off if I'd been wrong?"

"Can you tell us what happened that night?" Dean asked, giving Mark a warning look about angering the old man.

Watson glared at Mark a moment longer, then turned pointedly back to Dean. "I was outside, catching fireflies and putting 'em in a jar. You know, like ten-year-old boys do when they ain't got anything better to entertain 'em. There was a party going on inside the inn, a birthday party for the twins. My mama was working, serving food and cleaning up after the guests. She was real happy that night, because Ian would take over the next day and he'd promised her a raise."

Sighing, Watson continued, "Anyway, I heard some voices out by the old caretaker's shack, so I snuck up to see what was going on. I knew nobody ought to be there. I heard Charles and Felcher and Tagert talking about their operation. Tagert was saying they were going to have to quit. The cops were getting too close, he said. I heard him say that killing the revenue officer was a big mistake. They were going to get caught. Buck didn't seem to care one way or the other. He was gripin' about something else. Probably wanted more money.

"They heard someone outside and they all froze. From where I was hiding, I could see that it was Ian and Mary Anna coming up the path. I wanted to warn 'em, but before I could decide how to do it without tipping Charles off that I'd heard him talking, all hell broke loose. Mary Anna said something to Tagert, I can't recall what. And then Charles shot Ian. Just shot him, cold."

Dean shivered, imagining the moment. Anna's horror when she saw her beloved brother fall.

Watson drew a long, shaky breath, as though reliving the moment in his life-weary mind. "Tagert started yelling at Charles, but Charles shot Anna before anyone could stop him. I went numb then. Couldn't have moved if I wanted to. Next thing I knew, Charles shot Buck. Whether it was 'cause he was a witness to the murders, or because he'd been causing a stink about the money, I never really knew."

Mark looked up from his notes. "This is . . . incredible," he said, his voice a bit unsteady.

"It's true," Watson insisted. "Every damn word of it."

"We believe you, Bill," Dean said gently. "I already suspected something like this."

Bill nodded. "I sat there without moving, scared that if I moved, they'd shoot me just like they had the others. There was a lot of noise going on inside the inn, so it took a while for the guests to figure out what had happened. By that time, Charles had told Tagert exactly what to say. Tagert was mad, and scared spitless, I think, but Charles kept telling him they'd had no choice. He said all they had to do was stick together and their troubles would be over. The cops could close the case on the other murder, and he and Tagert could retire with the money they'd already made with their bootlegging. Charles ran back to the inn, then came back with his daddy to 'witness' the tragedy."

"You mean, Charles killed the twins because he needed someone to blame for the Prohibition officer's murder? Not because they were to take over the inn the next day?" Mark asked, looking dazed as he tried to follow the story.

"Charles never cared a lick about that inn," Watson said, "but he had no intention of going to jail for any of his money-making schemes. He never did like Ian, and he knew there were plenty of others who didn't, either. He figured if Tagert backed him up, everyone would believe that Ian had been the real criminal in the family. Besides, the twins had caught him meeting with Buck and Tagert. Wouldn't have taken them long to figure out what was really goin' on that night."

Watson looked back at Dean as he continued, "They called the police chief, a lazy, crooked cop who'd been on the take for years, and hated Ian Cameron, anyway. He swallowed the whole story. If he ever suspected anything different, he never breathed a word. Charles probably paid him off. He retired a few months later, then Tagert died in that so-called hunting accident—"

"Charles killed him," Dean murmured.

"More than likely. By that time, my mama had been fired and we was living in Hot Springs, trying to scratch out enough of a living to keep us fed and clothed."

"You said Charles threatened you and your mother," Dean reminded him. "Did you confront him that night?"

"He saw me," Watson said grimly. "When he come back with all those people to provide him an alibi, he spotted me sitting in the bushes and I guess he figured I'd been there all along. He slipped into my bedroom that night—I was laying awake, trying to get up the courage to tell someone what I seen. He had a knife in his hand. Told me he'd cut me into pieces if I said a word, and then he'd go after my mama."

"That son of a bitch," Mark muttered. "You were just a boy."

"He made his point. I kept my mouth shut, even when his daddy fired my mama. He told her they couldn't afford us anymore, what with the scandal and all."

"When did you start the blackmail?" Mark asked, unable to keep the disapproval out of his voice.

Watson gave a bark of laughter that held little humor. "I was twenty-five. My mama was dead, worked herself to death thanks to those coldhearted Peavys. I was barely getting by. Charles Peavy was founding his fortune on reasonably honest investments with capital he'd made from his bootlegging days. I'd had to live with the horror of that night all those years. I didn't see nothing fair about it. So I went to him and told him he owed me. Owed me big. Told him I wanted a guaranteed lifetime job with his family, at a decent rate of pay. Told him if he'd take care of me for life, the way my mama was promised, I'd keep my mouth shut."

"How could you do that?" Dean asked, unable to hold his own opinions back any longer. "Because you kept quiet, Charles Peavy got away with murder. Several murders."

"If I'd talked then, there'd have been two more dead. Me and my ma," Watson snarled. "No one would've thought twice about us. We was just the servants, after all."

"But later—"

Watson sighed and shrugged one bony shoulder. "By then, I just didn't care no more. I was old enough and had seen enough of the rough side of life that he couldn't scare me. I told him I wouldn't go as easy as the twins did. Told him I had a letter with a friend that was to be sent to all the newspapers if anything happened to me. Told him that same friend would make damned sure I was avenged. Charles didn't dare cross me. He set me to doing odd jobs for his wife, and I stayed on with them and their kids for the next fifty years."

"You mean the entire Peavy family was in on this secret? Even the younger ones?" Mark asked incredulously.

"'Course not." Watson gave Mark a look of dislike. "Charles told 'em I was to stay on because of their family honor, or some such nonsense. He wrote in his will that I was to be supported for the rest of my natural life. Wasn't a damned thing they could do about it, though none of 'em liked it much. Only one who ever knew the truth, far as I know, was Charles's girl. Margaret. The snootiest, orneriest woman I ever had the dishonor of knowing. Took after her father, that one did."

Mark dropped his pen. He retrieved it hastily. "Margaret *knew?*"

"Told her myself," Watson said with some satisfaction. "She got to bad-mouthing me one day, telling me she was getting rid of me whatever it took and that there weren't nothing I could do about it, since her daddy was dead. I told her the truth about her precious daddy. Told her I'd ruin her in town. Since she liked playing the grand lady around Destiny, she didn't dare call my bluff. She hated me, but she made sure the money kept coming."

"And now you are telling the truth," Dean said.

Watson laughed shortly. "Sure as hell am. And I want you to print every word of it," he ordered Mark. "Serve the snotty bitch right to have everyone know where her sacred money came from."

"I'm not sure I *can* print this," Mark demurred. "This is all just hearsay. Your word against the Peavys."

"How stupid you think I am, boy?" Watson glared at Dean. "Get that big Bible off my nightstand. Glued inside the back cover, you'll find a letter in Charles Peavy's own hand. You can have his signature verified. It tells everything he done."

"How on earth did you get him to do that?" Dean asked, stunned.

Watson's smile wasn't pleasant. "I was holding a knife at the time. Told him that if he didn't do what I said, I'd cut him into little pieces. And then I'd go after his baby son, his little Gaylon. He believed me. I'd learned from the best, you see."

Shaken, Dean clutched the ragged Bible in his left hand. The whole story made him sick. Ian and Anna had been the only true innocents involved, he realized sadly.

Watson motioned toward Dean's sling with a frail, shaky hand. "You tangle with the Peavys already?"

Dean nodded curtly. "I think so."

"They won't be bothering you after this. Wouldn't dare."

Dean hoped the old man was right. He hated every minute of this, but he knew the Cameron name had to be cleared.

Even if it happened seventy-five years too late.

Watson looked suddenly tired. Sick. Very, very old. "I ain't saying I'm proud of anything I've done. But maybe this will make up for some of it. If you see them ghosts again, you tell 'em—you tell 'em—"

His voice faded.

Dean sighed. "I'll tell them you finally told the truth."

Watson closed his eyes. "That'll do. Or maybe I'll be telling 'em myself before very long."

Dean and Mark glanced at each other. Mark looked as dazed as Dean felt.

"Get out of here," Watson muttered. "I'm tired. Anything else you want to know, it's all in that letter. Take the book with you. Never done me much good, anyway."

Dean and Mark left without saying anything.

There was really nothing left to say.

11

They that love beyond the world cannot be separated by it.

—William Penn

DEAN WAS LOST in his own thoughts during the hour-and-a-half ride back to Destiny. The old Bible lay in his lap. Within its covers lay the proof of Ian and Mary Anna's innocence. His satisfaction at finally clearing their names was almost overwhelmed by his grief that his success would take Anna forever beyond his reach.

Mark left Dean to his thoughts; Mark, too, seemed to be preoccupied with the story they'd heard from the bitter, dying old man. They had almost reached the Destiny city limits when Mark broke the taut silence.

"You've seen them, haven't you?" he asked quietly. "The ghosts, I mean."

Dean's fingers tightened around the Bible. "What makes you ask?" he countered.

Mark gave him a chiding look. "Can't you just tell me the truth?"

Dean hesitated a moment, then shrugged. "If I tell you, you have to promise to keep it quiet. I don't want anyone else to know my lead came from a ghost, all right? I, er, I have my business future to consider."

"Mary Anna," Mark said without commenting on Dean's request.

Dean didn't ask how Mark knew which of the twins he'd talked to. "Yes."

"Damn." Mark shook his head, looking even more dazed than he had by Watson's revelations. "What the hell is going on here?"

"I wish I could tell you, Mark." Dean looked out the window again, thinking of the coming separation from Anna. "I wish I understood it myself," he added wistfully.

Why *had* he been the one chosen to help the twins? Why had he finally discovered true love with a woman he couldn't have? And why did it have to hurt so damn much?

Mark parked in front of the inn, but made no move to get out of the car. "I don't think I'll come in," he said. "I want to go home, have a stiff drink and try to process everything I've learned today."

Dean didn't urge Mark to stay. He had his own mission to accomplish. One he dreaded, even as he anticipated the pleasure in Anna's dark eyes at having the truth finally revealed.

"You *are* going to print the article?" he asked as he reached for his door handle with his left hand.

Mark nodded. "I'll print it, as soon as I decide how to word it."

Dean left the Bible lying in his seat. "You'll need the letter," he said, nodding toward the old book. "You'll want to have it verified first, maybe get a few experts to comment on it. Make copies and spread them around for insurance. I'll be calling on Margaret Vandover this evening."

"I know how to do my job." The slight curtness of Mark's tone told of his weariness, the strain of what lay ahead for him. For both of them.

Dean winced. "I know. I didn't mean to imply otherwise. Sorry if it sounded as though I did."

Mark nodded, appeased. "I'll keep you updated on my progress."

"Thanks. And, uh, Mark. Be careful."

"I should be saying that to you."

They both knew that Margaret was aware of the truth. Had she hired someone to warn Dean off, or had she shared her knowledge with someone else in the family who'd vowed to keep it buried?

That was something Dean figured he'd find out before long, one way or another. At the moment, he didn't even care.

He needed to see Anna.

AUNT MAE was waiting in the newly remodeled lobby when Dean entered the inn, standing behind the buffed and polished reception desk as though he were an arriving guest. "So you and Mark are back from your mysterious mission," she commented. "Were you successful?"

"Yes. I'll tell you all about it this evening," he promised her, thinking how very patient she'd been with him during the past weeks, despite her obvious worry.

It was typical of her that she didn't press him for details. "You look tired," was all she said as she rounded the end of the desk and approached him. "Is your arm hurting?"

It was throbbing dully, but it couldn't compare with the pain centered in Dean's chest. "It's fine."

"Maybe you should get some rest."

"You're probably right," he agreed, trying not to sound too eager to be alone. "I'll be in my room if you need me."

She nodded, watching him closely. She laid one hand on his good arm before he could move away. "Dean? Are you going to be all right?" she asked, deep concern in her eyes.

He kissed her soft cheek. "Sure I will, Aunt Mae," he said heartily, knowing he was lying. "Aren't I always?"

He felt her watching him as he left the lobby, but he didn't dare risk looking back.

He was concerned that she might read the truth in his eyes, and know that he *wasn't* all right. That he might never be all right again.

He stopped by the vacant sitting room on his way to his bedroom. Anna wasn't there, or at least, she didn't appear to him if she was.

Running his left hand through his hair, he headed for his room, his steps heavy. He was certain she would come to him there.

Anna would be impatient to hear what he'd learned, he reasoned. She would be delighted that Mark planned to write the article clearing hers and Ian's reputation.

Dean wished he could be a little happier that he'd done this for her. Happy that justice had been served after all this time, and that he'd played a vital role. But all he could think about was Anna's certainty that she and her brother would be freed when their names were cleared.

He had to believe she was right. Why else would they have remained here for so long, when the others before and after them had all gone on?

He hoped he'd have a chance to tell her goodbye. To touch her one last time. To feel her cool lips beneath his. To tell her how much he would miss her. How he would never forget her. Never stop loving her.

She wasn't in his room.

"Anna?" he called cautiously, looking around. Was she there, watching him?

"Anna, I've found what you've been hoping for. Mark and I have proof that you and Ian were murdered. That you were innocent."

There was no response.

He looked at the corner where the empty chair sat, his shirt from the night before still draped over it. It was only a chair. Only a shirt.

"Anna?" he said again, turning away from the corner and looking toward the bed where she'd come to him, kissed him, showed her concern for him. "Are you here? I want to tell you what Watson said."

The room was silent. Dean sensed that he was alone. Anna wasn't there. Would she ever be again?

He sank to the edge of the bed, his head bent, his right arm drawn tightly against his body, the pain of his injury merging with the aching of his heart.

"Anna," he whispered. "Don't leave me like this."

DEAN HALF EXPECTED Margaret to refuse to see him when he showed up at her door that evening. Though he was prepared to fight his way in, if necessary, it didn't come to that. He was escorted into her parlor by a coolly courteous housekeeper.

He found Margaret sitting in a fragile-looking antique chair, flanked by her son, the mayor, and her nephew, the chief of police.

Dean looked from Margaret to Charles to Roy. "Well?" he asked dryly. "Where's the senator?"

"Gaylon is at his home in Little Rock," Margaret replied briskly. "I saw no need for him to be involved in this."

Dean cocked his head curiously, trying to read the woman's expression. "You act as though you were expecting me."

She nodded. "I was. I received a call this afternoon from Bill Watson. He was . . . delighted that you'd visited him. He wanted me to know the details of your conversation."

"I wish someone would tell me what the hell is going on here," Mayor Charles Vandover complained, looking from his mother to Dean. "Why did you go see old Bill, Gates? What is this vendetta you have against my family?"

"I have nothing against your family, Mayor," Dean replied. He hadn't been asked to sit down, so he remained standing, his good arm at his side, the other resting in the white sling across his chest. "Or at least, I had nothing against any of you until someone dropped a potting bench on me and almost killed me."

Chief Roy Peavy jumped up from his seat. "What the *hell* are you talking about?" he demanded, the loud, officious voice incongruous with his mousy appearance. "You aren't blaming us for your own damn-fool carelessness, are you?"

"I wasn't careless. I was deliberately attacked. And yes, I think someone in your family was behind it." Dean looked at Margaret again. "How much do they know?" he asked her.

She looked almost as old as Watson had earlier, though Dean knew she was nearly twenty years younger than the man. "Nothing," she admitted. "I'm the only one who knows the truth."

"So you're the one—"

"I asked that you be warned about interfering with my family business," she cut in flatly. "I never intended for you to be seriously injured."

"Who was he?"

"The son of a man who once worked for me," Margaret replied with a resigned sigh. "He has a rather long record, and he isn't particular about how he comes by the money to support his habits. It wasn't the first time I'd had him do a favor for me."

Charles also rose from his chair, staring at Margaret incredulously. *"Mother?"*

"Please sit down, Charles. You, too, Roy. This won't take long."

Margaret drew a deep breath. Dean noticed that she still hadn't invited him to take a chair. "How much is it going to take to keep you quiet?" she asked him coolly.

He narrowed his eyes. "You think that's why I'm here?"

She shrugged delicately. "Why else? As you pointed out, you have no reason to hate me, no reason to want to humiliate me and my family in this town because of something that happened long before you arrived. You heard something that made you suspect the truth and you figured you could make some money from it, just as Bill Watson did for all those years. I've had you investigated, Gates. I know you've put every penny you own into that worthless old inn. Obviously, you think you've found a way to recoup some of your investment."

"Mother, what the hell is this all about?" Charles demanded. "What does Gates have to do with Bill Watson?"

Margaret sighed. "I guess this man is going to make sure you know the truth. Maybe it's time you do. You'll probably have to support him the rest of his life because of it, just the way I've had to support Watson before him."

Dean folded his arms, waiting to hear what she'd tell her son.

"My father murdered Ian and Mary Anna Cameron, and Buck Felcher," she stated baldly. "He participated in an official cover-up and later killed Stanley Tagert, the crooked police officer who'd been in league with him. He then took the money he'd made through the sale of contraband merchandise and, through shrewd investments, made enough to establish himself and his heirs as prominent and powerful citizens of this area. Bill Watson knew the truth from the beginning. He blackmailed my father for years. I found out everything several years later, when it was my turn to pay for Watson's silence."

Charles and Roy seemed stunned.

Dean concentrated on Margaret. "You didn't care that two innocent people were murdered, that their reputations were ruined in their hometown?"

"I never knew them," Margaret stated simply. "I loved my father. He was a powerful, respected man in this town. How could I let his name be smeared by something that had happened years before I was born? He was already dead when I discovered the truth about him. The Camerons left no heirs, no one to suffer from their tragedy. I saw no purpose in letting the truth out."

"Did you deliberately cause trouble for Mark Winter when he began to research a book about the murders?"

Margaret hesitated. "I made it clear that the local citizens wouldn't care to have their dirty laundry aired in public through a book that cast our town in an unfavorable light."

She had a unique way of rationalizing her behavior, Dean thought wryly. She made it sound as though it hadn't been herself and her own family reputation she'd been protecting, but the entire population of the small town she and her kin had dominated for so many years.

Margaret glanced at Roy. "You'll say nothing about any of this, of course," she said. "I will pay for Mr. Gates's silence. And Mr. Winter's, as well, I presume."

"No," Dean said with a cold smile. "You won't. I'm not here for your money, Mrs. Vandover. I'm here to let you know that the whole truth will be printed in the *Destiny Daily*, exactly as Bill Watson told it to us. We have a letter from your father backing him up."

She paled. "You—you're printing the story?"

"Yes."

"But . . . but why? Don't you know what that will do to my family?"

Dean shrugged. His injured arm throbbed, reminding him that this woman did not deserve his sympathy. "Had you told the truth when you learned of it, rather than going to such extremes to hide it, your family wouldn't have suffered nearly as much," he said. "No one would have blamed you for your father's actions. Of course, no one would have named a library after him, either. Something tells me that name will be changed soon."

Anger flared in her eyes. "You do this and you'll regret it. I swear you will!"

"I'll take my chances."

After a long, taut moment, she wilted as she realized there was nothing more she could do to stop him.

"You'll destroy my father's name—and mine, as well—but I won't let you destroy my family."

She turned back to her nephew. "Mr. Gates will probably want to press charges against me," she said calmly. "You will cooperate with him if he does. You've been an honest officer of the law. No one will hold your grandfather's actions against you if you continue to do your job well. Nor the improvident behavior of your eccentric old aunt," she added with a touch of grim humor. "You make it clear you had nothing to do with this, you hear?"

"But, Aunt Margaret—"

"I won't be pressing charges," Dean said wearily. "I'm more than ready for this to be over. Destiny is my home, too, now. And I have an inn to restore."

Margaret brightened. "Does that mean—"

"Mark's working on an article now about the interview Watson gave us this afternoon," Dean cut in. "I want everyone to know the truth about the Cameron twins."

"Please don't try to tell me *you've* seen the ghosts," Margaret said, her lip curled, her disappointment at his determination to reveal the truth obvious.

"I'm the owner of the historic Cameron Inn," he returned steadily. "It's the only really honorable name in this whole mess. I want my future guests to know it."

"That's your only interest in this?" Charles asked skeptically.

"It's all you need to know," Dean replied.

Margaret held his gaze for a long moment, then allowed her own to waver. "Charles, please escort Mr. Gates to the door. And be polite. As Destiny's mayor, you must support our local business owners."

"Don't know what you think you've accomplished with this, Gates," Charles complained at the door as Dean prepared to step outside. "You're only going to embarrass my family. And for what? A seventy-five-year-old scandal."

"Not a scandal. Murder," Dean corrected him. "Your grandfather should have paid for what he did, even if it's only his place in the town's history that suffers."

Charles winced. "Damn. The gossip mongers will have a field day with this, especially those who have never liked my mother, anyway. When they find out she's known about this—"

"She's an old woman. She had nothing to do with the murders, though she shouldn't have kept up the blackmail payments to Bill Watson. I won't say anything about her hiring someone to attack me—unless, of course, she causes any further trouble for me or my friends."

"She won't," Charles muttered. "Can't say I'm ever going to like you after this, but none of us will give you any trouble. We'll be too busy trying to rebuild our own reputations."

"As your mother pointed out, no fair-minded person would blame any of you for your grandfather's actions. Your mother's behavior, on the other hand, is different. You and I both know I should be pressing charges against her. I could have been seriously hurt by her stunt, maybe even killed. As it is, I can tell you my arm hurts like hell."

"Have the medical bills sent to me," Charles said wearily. "I'll take care of them. And, Gates—thank you for not pressing charges."

"She's had to live with the knowledge that the father she adored was a murderer," Dean replied, his tone grim. "And now everyone else is going to know it. Maybe that's enough."

"Trust me, for my mother, there's nothing worse you could have done to her." The mayor saw Dean out, closed the door and then presumably returned to his mother's side.

ANNA WASN'T WAITING when Dean returned to the inn.

With a part of him constantly on the alert for any sign of her, Dean told the whole story to his aunt and Cara. Casey had already been tucked in for the night; it was almost midnight by the time Dean finished the long, complicated tale. He left out his encounters with Anna, saying only that he'd had a feeling from the beginning that something was missing from the legend. Something that had intrigued him.

He couldn't talk about Anna now. Maybe he never would.

"This is just fascinating, Dean," Mae breathed when Dean had completed the tale with the details of his visit that evening to Margaret Vandover. "You've solved a seventy-five-year-old mystery. Unmasked a murderer, even though he's already dead. You must feel like one of those fictional detectives you so love to read about."

Dean just felt tired. And empty. "It wasn't all that exciting, Aunt Mae. I simply did some research."

"And risked your life in the process," Cara said heatedly, looking at his sling. "I can't believe you let that mean old woman get away with hiring someone to attack you. She should go to jail for what she did to you, and so should the man who hurt you. Why, I—"

She stopped suddenly, her face going pale.

"What is it, Cara?" Dean asked.

"You, uh, wouldn't want me to testify, would you?" she asked in little more than a whisper. "I mean, I'm grateful to you for taking us in and for being so kind to us, and I'm very sorry you were hurt, but I simply couldn't appear in court. I—well, I just couldn't."

He wished he knew what Cara was hiding. What frightened her so badly. He hoped she would trust him enough someday to tell him. Maybe he will have regained enough energy by then to help her. For now, he let it go.

At the moment, he felt like a battered, fatigued, hopelessly lovesick male. Some hero, he thought with a private grimace.

Maybe he should leave Cara's problems alone. Or let Mark try to convince her to share them with him.

"I wouldn't expect you to testify, Cara," he promised quietly. "As I said, I'm not pressing charges against Margaret. As far as I'm concerned, it's over."

Over. The word echoed in his mind. *Was* it over? Was Anna already gone, her mission completed?

Had she left without even saying goodbye?

It was all he could do not to groan aloud at the thought.

"What about that old photograph we found, Dean?" Mae asked, her eyes gleaming with excitement. "Did you tell Mark about it? Is he going to run it with the article?"

"No," Dean said, more sharply than he'd intended. He couldn't bear the idea of making that photograph available for the morbidly curious. The photo would be all he had left of Anna; he wouldn't share it, not with anyone.

"I don't want the photograph mentioned, Aunt Mae," he added more gently. "I have my reasons, okay?"

"Whatever you say, dear," she murmured. Dean didn't miss the look that passed between her and Cara. Both of them then turned to him. The concern in their faces touched him, even as it made him restless.

"I think I'll go out for a walk," he said. "It's been a long day. I need to clear my mind with some fresh air."

To his relief, neither woman volunteered to accompany him. They must have sensed that he wanted to be alone.

No, that wasn't quite true. He didn't want to be alone.

He wanted—he needed—to be with Anna.

HE WALKED SLOWLY down the garden path, watching his steps in the darkness. He hadn't thought to bring a flashlight, but the full moon overhead gave just enough illumination for him to make his way in relative ease.

Midnight, he thought. February 14. Valentine's Day. It would have been Anna's one hundredth birthday. The thought made him shiver.

He hadn't worn a jacket. The frosty night breeze bit through his shirtsleeves. His breath hung in the air ahead of him.

He hardly noticed the cold. Only the silence.

The garden shed had been torn down the day after Dean had been injured in it. He paused at the place where it had been, staring glumly at the pile of rubble waiting to be hauled away. He mentally replayed Anna's frantic warning to him, the frightened, worried look in her eyes when she'd knelt beside him, sharing his suffering, despairing because she couldn't do more to help him.

He turned away and looked back toward the inn. There was a light burning in his bedroom window; he'd left the bedside lamp on. He remembered how Anna had come to him, had kissed his injuries and soothed his pain. How she'd left him wanting her with an ache that hadn't receded since.

An ache that would never be satisfied.

Pushing aside those disturbing memories, he walked on, to the end of the path where he'd first felt that cold, macabre feeling. The place where he'd turned and spotted Anna, looking at him with a plea for help in her haunted eyes.

He turned now, and saw nothing but the emptiness of the dark, winter-bare garden.

He let out a long, ragged breath and tipped his head back. His eyes closed, and his chest ached with a despair that was all new to him.

He was beginning to accept the fact that he might never see her again. That she was truly gone.

His grief was the fresh, tearing pain of loss. And it was all the more agonizing because he couldn't share it. His love had died in reality long before he was born; how could anyone else truly understand his mourning her now?

"Anna," he whispered, his throat raw. "Oh, God, Anna. I miss you."

"Dean?"

At first he thought her voice still echoed in his memories, soft and musical and muted. Like the sound of distant wind chimes.

And then she spoke again. "Dean."

He opened his eyes. She stood on the path in front of him, her white dress gleaming softly in the darkness, her face pale and solemn in the moonlight.

The relief was almost overwhelming. "Anna." He took a step closer, automatically reaching out to her with his left hand. "Anna—"

She placed her hand in his, that familiar sensation of cool marble felt through a thin, frustrating barrier. Again, he experienced those odd, rippling, strange-but-not-unpleasant tingles from their contact.

"Anna," he said again, drinking her in with his eyes. "I thought you weren't coming back."

Her smile was sad. "We know what you've done, Dean," she murmured, glancing up beside her. "We couldn't have left without telling you how much it means to us."

Dean followed her gaze. "Ian is with you?"

She nodded. "You still can't see him?"

"No."

She sighed. "I wish you could. He—we both want to thank you. And to tell you—" Her voice broke, but she continued gamely. "To tell you goodbye."

Dean had wanted the chance to say goodbye. But his pain at hearing the word was so great, he wondered if he could take this, after all.

He wasn't ready to let her go.

His fingers tightened instinctively around Anna's hand, as though he would hold her with him through sheer determination. "I—"

He choked, unable to speak around the lump that had formed in his throat.

With her free hand, she brushed her fingertips against his cheek in that tender gesture that had already become so sweetly familiar to him.

"You're a very special man, Dean Gates," she whispered, her dark eyes shining in the moonlight. "I can't imagine that anyone else would have done for us what you've done. You risked so much. Few others would have cared enough to have tried. How can we ever thank you?"

"All I did was keep asking questions until someone finally answered them," he managed to say evenly enough. "Now everyone will know the truth about you."

"And Ian," she reminded him.

He glanced at that eerily empty place beside her. He pictured a dark, temperamental young man, and nodded. "Ian, too."

"I know you'll do well with our inn, Dean," Anna murmured. Again, she gave him that sad-edged smile. "I have a feeling about it."

His chest tightened. "Anna—"

"I think we should go now. It—it will only hurt more if we stay longer."

He didn't release her. "Do you feel . . . different?" he asked awkwardly. "Do you know where you're going?"

"No," she whispered, looking away. "But we've done what we've set out to do. As you said, everyone will know the truth about us. We—we don't belong here. It's your home now."

"I don't know if I can stay here without you," he said roughly. "Everywhere I look, every room I enter, I'll think of you. I'll watch for you. And I'll miss you. God, how I'll miss you!"

Her fingers flexed convulsively in his grasp. She looked up at him, her lovely face distressed. "You have to stay! You have to take care of our home. You promised me."

"Don't you understand, Anna? I don't care about any of that now. Only you."

He lifted her hand to his lips. "If only I could go with you," he muttered against her palm.

She stroked his hair with her free hand. It felt as though a playful breeze had ruffled the heavy strands. "No, Dean," she said softly. "Don't say that. You have your whole life ahead of you. Your family, the inn. You should fall in love, have children—"

"No," he groaned, interrupting her. The images she evoked with her words—things he hadn't even known he wanted until then—were too painful to even contemplate. There would be no other woman. No children. Not for him.

Not without Anna.

He looked at her, making no effort to hide his raw emotions. "I love you. I'll always love you."

"Dean," she said brokenly. "Don't. I—I can't—"

He kissed her palm, her fingertips. Her lips.

"I love you," he said again. "God, how I wish—" He couldn't finish.

She seemed to understand. "So do I," she said, her icy cheek pressed to his. "Oh, Dean, I would give anything to stay here with you. But not like this. Not—not existing in different worlds. It isn't fair to you. To either of us."

He lifted his head, wondering if she was saying what it sounded like. "You would stay, if you could? Here, with me? Even—" He took a quick, deep breath, groping for a way to define the depth of her sincerity. "Even if it meant leaving your brother?"

Her eyes glittered brightly, as though filled with unseen tears. She didn't look at that space beside her, didn't take her gaze from Dean.

"Yes, God help me," she whispered. "Even if that was the choice I had to make. As much as I love Ian, I would stay with you. But—"

"Tell me," he ordered her, desperately needing to hear the words, if only just this once. "Tell me what you feel."

"I love you," she said, her voice clear, certain. "I love you more than I've ever loved before. I never knew love could be like this. It's just the way my mother told me it would be."

Swallowing hard, Dean rested his forehead against hers. "Your mother got her wish, after all. You found true love."

"Yes," she said, her voice breaking. "Yes. If only—I wish—"

He drew her closer, ignoring the twinge of protest from his injured arm.

Her cheek pressed hard against his. Her fingers entwined tightly with his own. Their heartache was an almost palpable force surrounding them, binding them together.

Dean had never understood that love could be this glorious. Or that it could hurt so very badly.

12

Over the mountains and over the waves,
Under the fountains and under the graves . . .
Love will find out the way.

—Anonymous

IT HAPPENED so quietly, so subtly that at first Dean didn't realize that anything had changed. And then he felt it. A strange, pulsing warmth. It seemed to begin in Anna's fingertips. Slowly—so very slowly, it spread.

Still holding her hand, he lifted his head to look at her. Wide-eyed, she stared up at him, his own questions reflected in her stunned expression.

Her hand grew warmer. Softer.

It was as if the unseen barrier between them was being slowly peeled away.

Her hand no longer felt as though it were made of marble. It wasn't cold. It wasn't lifeless.

Hardly daring to breathe, Dean released her fingers to lift his hand to her face. Cupping her cheek in his palm, he brushed his thumb against her lower lip.

Her skin felt flushed, heated. Her lips soft. Tremulous. Damp.

He felt warm breath against his flesh.

He was dizzy. So scared, so hopeful, he was shaking like a leaf.

Very slowly, he lowered his fingertips to her throat.

And felt the pulse beating there, rapid, but steady.

"Dean?" she whispered, and even her voice had changed. She sounded so close. So startled.

So very real.

She drew back from him and looked down at herself. He followed her gaze. Her white dress was dirty at the hem. He'd never seen dirt on it before. Beneath the lace-trimmed bodice, her small, perfect breasts rose and fell.

Breathing.

"Anna." He whispered her name, still afraid to accept what seemed to be happening. Knowing it would kill him if he allowed himself to believe, only to find out he'd been mistaken.

She spread her hands in confusion, still looking downward. "I feel—Dean, I'm—"

Impatiently, she shook her head. Her dark hair ruffled against her cheek with the movement. A stray breeze caught a loose strand, tossing it into her eyes. She reached up to brush it back, her movements rather awkward.

"I don't know what has happened," she said, looking at him with eyes that shone now with hope, with the anticipation of joy. "But I think—oh, Dean, I think I'm alive. *Really* alive."

"Anna!" Unable to hold back any longer, he pulled his injured arm from its supportive sling and reached for her. If there was pain, he ignored it. All he felt was the warmth and softness of her slender body, held tightly against his chest.

Her arms went around his neck. Her mouth locked with his. The kiss was hard. Hot. Shattering.

She broke it off with a gasping sound that could have been a laugh or a sob. "I can feel you," she cried, pressing more closely against him. "You're strong and you're solid and so very, very warm. You feel *wonderful!*"

"So do you," he managed to say, his hands running feverishly over her.

Every inch of her felt real. Perfect. Alive.

Alive! The word reverberated in his head. He didn't know how, but he knew—somehow he knew without doubt—that it was true. Anna was alive. And in his arms. And he was never letting her go.

"I love you," he said, kissing her roughly, repeatedly. "I love you."

She returned kiss for kiss, as eager and hungry as he. "I love you," she said whenever he gave her a chance to speak. "I love you so much."

"Stay with me. Promise you'll stay with me."

"For the rest—" Her voice broke, then steadied. "For the rest of my life," she vowed. "However long that may be."

"I love you." He murmured the words against her lips, then smothered her reply with his kiss.

It was a long time before Anna drew back. "Ian," she said on a gasp. "I almost—"

Pulling out of Dean's arms, she whirled. "Ian!" she said, apparently seeing something—someone—Dean did not. "Isn't it wonderful? Aren't you—Ian?"

Dean watched Anna closely. She took a step away from him, toward the brother that only she could see.

Her expression was suddenly anguished. "Ian, you aren't—Ian, *no!*"

She launched herself forward. Dean caught her in his good arm when she would have stumbled.

She clung to him, limp, dazed, still gazing longingly at that empty spot.

"Please. Don't go," she whispered to her brother. "Stay with me. With *us*. Please. Stay—"

A faint whisper of sound lifted the hairs on the back of Dean's neck. He sensed, more than heard, the words.

"*. . . love you, Anna. Be happy.*"

"Ian," Anna said, sobbing, sagging against Dean's side. "Oh, Ian."

Holding her, Dean strained to see, but there was only darkness. Silence. "Is he—"

"He's gone," she whispered. "He just . . . faded away from me. I—I can't see him now. I can't . . . hear him."

Dean held her close as she wept. Her tears were hot and wet against his throat.

This, too, was a part of being alive, he musedly poignantly. Joy, grief, passion, heartache, laughter and pain. It was only love that made it all worthwhile.

Anna didn't cry long. Dean didn't think she was the type who would shed tears often. Taking a deep, ragged breath, she drew back and wiped her face with the back of one hand.

"He's gone," she said. "Maybe it was meant to be this way. His name has been cleared and I—I've found you."

She touched Dean's cheek with her wet, warm fingers.

He caught her hand in his. "Regrets?" he asked.

"I'll miss Ian," she murmured. "I'll always miss him. It's as if—as if a part of me has been torn away. But . . . no. I have no regrets, Dean. I love you. If I had to make the choice again—" She swallowed, then finished in a whisper. "It would still be you."

He drew her close and kissed her, trying to soothe her sorrow with his love.

After a moment, she put her arms around his neck and kissed him back. And he knew she would be all right.

Mary Anna Cameron was meant to savor every moment of life. Through her, Dean would learn to savor it, too.

IT WAS VERY LATE when Dean and Anna slipped into the inn, hand in hand. The others had gone to bed, probably still presuming Dean needed time alone.

Both almost giddy with emotion, Dean and Anna closed themselves in his room, trying to be quiet. They didn't turn on the overhead light; the soft illumination from the bedside lamp was enough for them then.

"How will we ever explain who I am?" she asked, turning to him in question.

"We'll think of something," he assured her, reaching for her. "Later."

She slid her arms around his neck. Her hand lingered at the thick bandages protecting his stitches. "Your arm," she murmured, pressing a kiss on his neck, just above the injury. "You mustn't strain it. You'll pull the stitches out."

She felt so good in his arms. So slim and supple and sweet. "I don't care," he murmured, his mouth hovering over hers.

"Well, I do," she said firmly. "It's my job now to take care of you. Starting tonight."

He laughed softly. "You're living in the nineties now, Anna. Women don't 'take care' of their men the way they used to."

She frowned. "People still fall in love in the nineties, do they not?"

"I assume that they do. Some of them, anyway."

"Then they should take care of each other," she pronounced. "That's what love is all about."

He figured they would have plenty of time to discuss the changing roles of women in the late twentieth century. He would make time for long, leisurely walks, for philosophical discussions, for anything important to her.

Perhaps he'd neglected his first wife, put his work and everything else ahead of her in his life. He would never do that with Anna.

He had come so close to losing her forever. He would never take her for granted, no matter how busy he became with his—with *their*—inn.

"I love you, Anna," he said evenly, holding her gaze with his own.

Her face softened. She lifted a hand to his cheek. "I love you, Dean. With all my heart."

He threaded the fingers of his left hand through her dark hair. It was soft and thick, and it curled around his fingers.

Her eyelashes curled, too, he noticed, long and lush and naturally dark. There were three freckles across the bridge of her small, perfect nose. She had a dimple at the left corner of her full mouth.

He would never grow tired of studying her, learning every centimeter of her. Beginning tonight.

"Anna," he murmured, brushing his lips across hers. "I want you."

Her cheeks darkened with a flush. He touched them, relishing the faint heat. "I want you, too," she said steadily, holding his gaze with hers.

He would have liked to sweep her into his arms and carry her to his bed. Considering that he'd probably bust a dozen stitches and bleed all over her if he did, he'd better wait until a better time for that particular romantic gesture, he decided wryly. Instead, he took her hand in his good one and led her to the mattress.

He ran his finger across the high neckline of her white dress, noting the delicacy of the fabric, the fragile daintiness of the lace. He'd seen dresses like this in vintage shops, and knew it would be worth a great deal to a collector. But all he cared about now was getting it out of the way. "How does this unfasten?"

She smiled. "I hardly remember."

He kissed her nose, her cheek, the dimple at the left corner of her mouth. "Think hard," he suggested, his voice growing rough.

She giggled softly and reached up with both hands. Despite her disclaimer, she unfastened the dress easily enough. Shyly, she lowered the bodice, baring the creamy tops of her small breasts.

Almost reverently, Dean kissed her there. So soft, he thought with a groan. So warm. So incredibly beautiful.

"Dean?" Anna's voice was a shaken whisper.

"Mmm?"

"I—I hope you don't mind too badly, but I—I'm not a virgin," she said in a brave rush. "Jeffrey and I—two times, we—"

He shushed her by placing a finger over her lips. "I hope *you* don't mind, but I'm not a virgin, either," he said. "I was married, Anna."

She smiled rather sheepishly. "I know that."

He didn't return the smile. "The past doesn't matter. Somehow, we've found each other. And all I care about is our future—together."

Her eyes gleamed in the lamplight. "I love you."

"I love you."

"Make me yours."

"Yes," he said hoarsely, drawing her close. "Mine. And I'm yours. Forever, Anna."

With surprising ease, he removed her dress, her tiny sandals, her sheer stockings and quaint undergarments. He would study them and marvel over them later; for now, he had eyes only for her. His own clothes fell in a careless heap on the floor.

There wasn't an inch of her he missed in his lovingly thorough exploration. The pulsing hollow of her throat. Her firm, coral-tipped breasts. Her sleek, flat stomach. A small, round mole at her waist. Her thighs. The softness between them.

She writhed beneath him on the bed, protesting only when she worried that he would hurt his arm. He felt the occasional tug at his stitches, but any discomfort was overwhelmed by the exhilaration of loving Anna.

Anna cooperated fully while he learned her body, her fingers clenching in the sheets beneath her as she arched and writhed, biting back her cries of pleasure.

And then she pressed Dean gently back into the pillows and began her own extensive exploration of his body, always careful of his injured arm. His teeth clenched, his muscles rigid, his skin damp and exquisitely sensitized, Dean wondered dazedly if he would survive the night.

The time finally came when he could wait no longer to be inside her. He rolled her onto her back, settling himself between her thighs.

"Your arm, Dean," she whispered, her voice hoarse with her own need. "Please be careful."

"Forget the arm. I need you, Anna."

"Yes. I need you, too, Dean. I need—" Her words broke off in a gasp when he surged inside her.

She was hot and wet and tight, and when he joined with her, Dean knew he had never been truly alive until that moment.

He and Anna were one. Somehow, they had always been one, even when time and space and death, itself, had separated them.

IT WAS A LONG TIME LATER before they slept. Anna lay snuggled against Dean's left side, her head on his shoulder, her bare, still-damp body entwined with his. His right arm throbbed, but he ignored the discomfort, choosing, instead, to savor the pleasure.

"Marry me, Anna," he whispered into her hair.

She stirred. "But how—"

"We'll work it out, somehow. Just say you'll marry me."

He felt her smile against his skin. "I'll marry you."

"Good. By the way, did you know it's your birthday?"

She lifted her head in surprise. "It is? Now?"

"Yes. It's after midnight on the fourteenth. Happy Valentine's Day, Anna. And happy birthday."

She groaned and lay back down. "I don't even want to think about how old I am."

He laughed softly. "We'll start counting again at twenty-six. Oh, man," he added, suddenly dazed all over again. "I'm still having a little trouble believing this."

She murmured an agreement. "I know how you feel. It's very strange. But it's right."

"Yes. It's right." He kissed her. And then, content, he closed his eyes and nestled her closer. "I'm almost afraid to go to sleep," he murmured. "I'm afraid I'll wake up and you'll be gone."

She locked her arms around his neck, careful to avoid his bandages. "I'm not going anywhere, my love. Go to sleep. I'll be here when you wake up."

And she was.

ANNA'S WHITE DRESS was wrinkled and dirty, and she refused to put it on to meet his aunt. Dean dug out a clean black sweatsuit for her to wear. The shirt hung almost to her knees and the pants swallowed her, but the drawstring at the waist kept them in place. The elastic bands at the wrists and ankles made the garments blousy, but wearable. She wore a pair of his thick white socks in lieu of shoes. When she saw herself in the mirror, she laughed.

"Do I look like a modern woman—or a modern boy?" she asked, her slender figure all but hidden in the folds of his sweatsuit.

"You look adorable," Dean assured her, kissing the top of her head as he fastened the white cotton shirt he'd donned with a pair of jeans.

"Your family will think you've dragged home a vagabond."

"My family will love you, just as I do."

They had already prepared their story. Now it was time to test it. Anna couldn't remember ever being more nervous. She had to take several deep breaths for courage before she and Dean stepped out into the real world, with one last, wistful look at the bed where they'd spent such a magical night.

Mae and Cara and Casey were already seated at the dining-room table, having breakfast. "We thought you would want to sleep in this morning," Mae said, hearing the dining-room door swing open. "We—oh! Why, who—"

She stopped with a gasp, staring at Anna.

Anna's hand tightened convulsively in Dean's.

"Aunt Mae, Cara, Casey, this is Anna. My fiancée." Dean spoke as easily as though he were merely bidding them good morning.

Mae was on her feet, her face pale, her eyes fixed on Anna's with a mixture of fascination and disbelief. "Your—your fiancée?" she stammered. "But where? When? She looks like—"

Anna held her breath.

Dean never blinked. "Anna is the great-granddaughter of Nicholas Cameron, James Cameron's brother, who stayed in London when James emigrated to America. That would, of course, make her a distant cousin of the Cameron twins. She came here out of curiosity, wanting to know more about her American family and the tragedy that struck them."

"But—where did you meet? Where has she been staying? And you're *engaged?*" Aunt Mae looked a bit dizzy.

Anna stepped forward and placed her hand in the older woman's. "Please forgive us for springing this on you in such a way, Mrs. Harper," she said sincerely, trying to sound at least slightly British. "It's unforgivable of us, I know. Please believe that there were ... circumstances that kept me from meeting with you sooner. I love your nephew very much, and I want to spend the rest of my life making him happy. I know how close he is to you. I hope you can accept me into your family."

Mae's face softened. She took Anna's hand in both of hers. "Oh, my dear, of course. I was just taken by surprise, that's all. I'm thrilled that Dean has fallen in love—why, just look at him. It's written all over his face."

Anna studied Dean's face through tear-filled eyes. He grinned at her, looking as though he didn't care if his feelings were written on his face in permanent ink. He loved her. And he didn't care if everyone knew it.

What had she done, she wondered, to deserve this joy?

They spent the rest of the morning reciting the story they'd concocted so carefully, improvising when necessary.

Anna had told Dean earlier that she felt terrible about lying to his family, and he shared her qualms, but both of them had agreed that the only way they could hope to have a normal life together was to keep her true identity a secret, from everyone. Even Mae and Bailey.

"It's such a shame that all your luggage was lost," Mae fretted later. "Honestly, those airlines these days are so careless. We'll have to see about getting you something to wear. And, Dean, you make sure she is compensated for her loss, you hear? Even if you have to hire a lawyer."

"Yes," Anna agreed with a smile for Dean. "I'm afraid all I have is one dress and a pair of heeled slippers. I can hardly go around in those or Dean's sweatclothing all the time."

"Sweatclothing?" Mae repeated with a puzzled frown, then looked at the fleece garments Anna was wearing. "Oh, his sweatsuit."

"I have some jeans and tops you can wear while you shop for new clothes," Cara offered shyly. "Shoes, too. You and I look to be about the same size."

"How kind of you, Cara. Thank you." Touched, Anna smiled. She thought she and Cara would become friends. It was nice to have a friend in this strange, rather frightening new world.

Mark stopped by that afternoon with a first draft of the article he'd written about his bizarre interview with Bill Watson. Cara, as usual, conveniently busied herself in the kitchen after escorting Mark into the sitting room with the others.

Mark was introduced to Anna Cameron, and given the same story Mae and Cara had heard earlier. Though he seemed to accept it easily enough, he looked at Anna very closely, and then at Dean.

He didn't stay long. As he left, he shook Dean's hand, congratulated him on his engagement, and then murmured within Anna's hearing, "Something tells me I don't really want to know the truth about your lovely fiancée."

"Trust me," Dean said, clasping his friend's hand firmly, "it's better if you don't."

"That's what I thought. Umm, Dean—anything you need, er, you know, paperwork, certificates, whatever—well, I have sources."

"Thanks. I'll probably be giving you a call."

Mark nodded, gave Anna one last, curious look, then smiled. "It's been one hell of an adventure," he commented as he departed.

Dean smiled and drew Anna close to his side. "The adventure is just beginning," he said.

She smiled lovingly up at him.

DEAN AND ANNA WALKED in the garden that evening, just before dark. He wore a jacket, this time, and she was bundled into a coat that belonged to his aunt.

It would be spring soon, Dean mused, looking at the few plants that had survived his cleanup of the area. They would plant trees, flowers, rosebushes. The gardens would come to life again. He looked forward to seeing it.

They paused at the end of the path, near the old shack. Anna's eyes were shuttered, her expression pensive as she looked around, lost in memories.

Dean wrapped his good arm around her waist. "Are you okay?"

"Yes. I was just thinking—"

"Of Ian?"

She nodded. "Yes. I only wish I knew if he were still here, or if he's gone on to be with Mother. I can't bear to think of him being alone in the grayness."

"You'll see him again, Anna. Someday."

"I know," she said confidently. "Just as I know he would have wanted this for me. He always wanted me to be happy."

"And are you?"

She turned to him, her face lifted to his, glowing with a deep contentment Dean couldn't have missed. "Yes," she murmured. "I'm happy. I'm going to be your wife. The mother of your children. We'll have a wonderful life together, I just know it."

"You have a feeling," Dean teased her, his throat tight with emotion.

Her smile was radiant now. "Yes. I have a feeling. And my feelings are *always* right."

"I believe you. I've learned to believe in a great many things since you came into my life, Mary Anna Cameron."

There in the garden of their home, he kissed her. And he knew the most precious discovery he'd made was love. He would never doubt it again.

Epilogue

IT WAS a clear, late-summer night in the garden. A billion stars glittered brightly overhead, and the scent of fresh-blooming flowers hung heavily in the air.

There were lights burning in the windows of the inn. Recently opened for business, it wasn't quite full, but several of the rooms were occupied, and the increasingly popular dining room had just closed after a busy evening. Silhouetted against the curtains in one downstairs bedroom window, two shadows merged in what might have been a passionate kiss.

At the end of the garden path, a solitary figure stood looking at that window, his usually hard, firm mouth curved into a very faint smile. An owl hooted above him, undisturbed by his presence.

The light went out in the bedroom, leaving its occupants in the quiet intimacy of darkness.

Outside, the man nodded in what might have been satisfaction, turned and faded silently into the shadows.

Alone.

*   *   *   *   *

Be sure to watch for the sequel to
A VALENTINE WISH, *coming to Temptation in
the summer of 1996. Bailey Gates has a bad
habit of getting involved with guys loaded
down with emotional baggage. But even she
isn't ready to take on Ian Cameron's problems!*

UNLOCK THE DOOR TO GREAT ROMANCE
AT BRIDE'S BAY RESORT

Join Harlequin's new across-the-lines series, set in an exclusive hotel on an island off the coast of South Carolina.

Seven of your favorite authors will bring you exciting stories about fascinating heroes and heroines discovering love at Bride's Bay Resort.

Look for these fabulous stories coming to a store near you beginning in January 1996.

Harlequin American Romance #613 in January
Matchmaking Baby by Cathy Gillen Thacker

Harlequin Presents #1794 in February
Indiscretions by Robyn Donald

Harlequin Intrigue #362 in March
Love and Lies by Dawn Stewardson

Harlequin Romance #3404 in April
Make Believe Engagement by Day Leclaire

Harlequin Temptation #588 in May
Stranger in the Night by Roseanne Williams

Harlequin Superromance #695 in June
Married to a Stranger by Connie Bennett

Harlequin Historicals #324 in July
Dulcie's Gift by Ruth Langan

Visit Bride's Bay Resort each month wherever Harlequin books are sold.

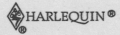

BBAYG

MILLION DOLLAR SWEEPSTAKES

SWP-H296

Are your lips succulent, impetuous, delicious or racy?

Find out in a very special Valentine's Day promotion—THAT SPECIAL KISS!

Inside four special Harlequin and Silhouette February books are details for THAT SPECIAL KISS! explaining how you can have your lip prints read by a romance expert.

Look for details in the following series books, written by four of Harlequin and Silhouette readers' favorite authors:

Silhouette Intimate Moments #691
Mackenzie's Pleasure by *New York Times* bestselling author Linda Howard

Harlequin Romance #3395
Because of the Baby by Debbie Macomber

Silhouette Desire #979
Megan's Marriage by Annette Broadrick

Harlequin Presents #1793
The One and Only by Carole Mortimer

Fun, romance, four top-selling authors, plus a FREE gift! This is a very special Valentine's Day you won't want to miss! Only from Harlequin and Silhouette.

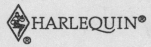

Women throughout time have
lost their hearts to:

Starting in January 1996, Harlequin Temptation
will introduce you to five irresistible, sexy rogues.
Rogues who have carved out their place in history,
but whose true destinies lie in the arms of
contemporary women.

#569 *The Cowboy*, Kristine Rolofson
(January 1996)

#577 *The Pirate*, Kate Hoffmann
(March 1996)

#585 *The Outlaw*, JoAnn Ross
(May 1996)

#593 *The Knight*, Sandy Steen
(July 1996)

#601 *The Highwayman*, Madeline Harper
(September 1996)

Dangerous to love, impossible to resist!

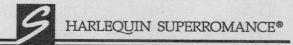

HARLEQUIN SUPERROMANCE®

From the bestselling author of
THE TAGGARTS OF TEXAS!
comes

THE CAMERONS OF COLORADO

Cupid, Colorado...

This is ranch country, cowboy country—a land of high mountains
and swift, cold rivers, of deer, elk and bear. The land is important
here—family and neighbors are, too. 'Course, you have the chance
to really get to know your neighbors in Cupid. Take the Camerons,
for instance. The first Cameron came to Cupid more than a hundred
years ago, and Camerons have owned and worked the Straight Arrow
Ranch—the largest spread in these parts—ever since.

For kids and kisses, tears and laughter, wild horses and wilder men—
come to the Straight Arrow Ranch, near Cupid, Colorado. Come meet
the Camerons.

THE CAMERONS OF COLORADO
by Ruth Jean Dale

Kids, Critters and Cupid (Superromance#678)
available in February 1996

The Cupid Conspiracy (Temptation #579)
available in March 1996

The Cupid Chronicles (Superromance #687)
available in April 1996

INTRODUCING...

A collection of award-winning books by award-winning authors! From Harlequin and Silhouette.

Heaven In Texas
by Curtiss Ann Matlock

National Reader's Choice Award Winner— Long Contemporary Romance

Let Curtiss Ann Matlock take you to a place called *Heaven In Texas*, where sexy cowboys in well-worn jeans are the answer to every woman's prayer!

"Curtiss Ann Matlock blends reality with romance to perfection!"
                                              —*Romantic Times*

Available this March wherever Silhouette books are sold.

Harlequin invites you to the
wedding of the century!

This April be prepared to catch the bouquet with
the glamorous debut of

Weddings by DeWilde

For years, DeWildes—the elegant and fashionable
wedding store chain—has helped brides around the
world turn the fantasy of their special day into reality.
But now the store and three generations of family are
torn apart by divorce. As family members face new
challenges and loves, a long-secret mystery begins to
unravel…. Set against an international backdrop of
London, Paris, New York and Sydney, this new series
features the glitzy, fast-paced world of designer wedding
fashions and missing heirlooms!

In April watch for:
SHATTERED VOWS
by Jasmine Cresswell

Look in the back pages of *Weddings by DeWilde* for
details about our fabulous sweepstakes contest to win a
real diamond ring!

Coming this April to your favorite retail outlet.

WBDT

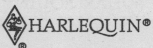

You're About to Become a Privileged Woman

Reap the rewards of fabulous free gifts and benefits with proofs-of-purchase from Harlequin and Silhouette books

Pages & Privileges™

It's our way of thanking you for buying our books at your favorite retail stores.

**Harlequin and Silhouette—
the most privileged readers in the world!**

For more information about Harlequin and Silhouette's PAGES & PRIVILEGES program call the Pages & Privileges Benefits Desk: 1-503-794-2499

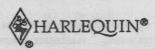

◆ HARLEQUIN®

HT-PP103